An Echo of Heaven presents an astonishingly fresh and penetrating portrait of a woman of independent character and strong physical appetites, looking for a way to understand the mystery of her life. It is a work by a Nobel Prize-winning writer at the height of his powers.

About the author: Kenzaburo Oe is his country's first truly modern writer, a revolutionary who has moved the Japanese novel out of a stagnant tradition into post-war world literature. He was born in Shikoku, the smallest of Japan's four main islands. After studying French literature at Tokyo University, he won his first literary award—the coveted Akutagawa Prize—for a short story, "The Catch," when he was twenty-three. During the anti-Security Treaty riots of 1960, he went to Peking as a representative of young writers, and a year later he traveled to Russia and Western Europe, where he came to know Sartre, whom he acknowledges as a major influence at the time.

His first novel to appear in English (1968) was *A Personal Matter*, an account of a man confronting the birth of a severely handicapped child. This was followed by *The Silent Cry, Teach Us to Outgrow Our Madness, The Pinch Runner Memorandum*, and *Nip the Buds, Shoot the Kids*—all of which, besides a number of other novels, have been translated into various foreign languages. His achievements as a writer committed to both literary and humanitarian causes were recognized in 1994 when he was awarded the Nobel Prize for Literature.

Oe, whose handicapped son Hikari has become a successful composer, lives in Tokyo with his wife and two other children.

AN ECHO OF HEAVEN

KENZABURO OE

TRANSLATED BY MARGARET MITSUTANI

KODANSHA INTERNATIONAL
TOKYO • NEW YORK • LONDON

Editorial note: Although it appears Western in its romanized form, "Marie" is a fairly common Japanese name with three syllables, pronounced roughly like the French word "marié."

Originally published by Shinchosha in 1989 under the title *Jinsei no shinseki*.

Distributed in the United States by Kodansha America, Inc., 575 Lexington Avenue, New York, N.Y. 10022, and in the United Kingdom and continental Europe by Kodansha Europe Ltd., 95 Aldwych, London WC2B 4JF. Published by Kodansha International Ltd., 17-14 Otowa 1-chome, Bunkyo-ku, Tokyo 112-8652, and Kodansha America, Inc.

First edition, 1996
Paperback edition, 2000
ISBN 4-7700-2505-X

00 01 02 03 04 05   10 9 8 7 6 5 4 3 2 1

AN ECHO OF HEAVEN

I

I recently received this letter from a young friend:

A while ago I came across the line "There have been men who loved the future like a mistress" in an essay by an Irish poet. The main point here is "men who loved the future," and "like a mistress" is just a metaphor he used to clarify the meaning. But when I read that line, it reminded me of us working together around the tent in Sukiyabashi Park, and both images took me back to that time. The three of us were young then, and there was only one woman, but no one tried to claim her for himself. We were all crazy about her, or devoted to her, if you like—loving her as we loved our own future.... Yes. That's how it was, I thought, looking back. In terms of the film we're making now: we want to start by showing the image of a beautiful woman, and three younger men, and that wholesome kind of love they have for her. They'll be smiling as they work. The smiles come naturally, because they're working with a beautiful woman, but they're also in love with their own future, and that's what keeps the

smiles from fading. If we can show all that in one scene, I think
we'll have got it right. The warm light that hovered about her
like a butterfly as she stood by that tent has set the tone for all the
work we've done with Asao so far. I'm hoping that will also be
true of this film. Even if the subject matter and the situation
we're working in make things hard.

The letter came from Guadalajara, Mexico. In sending it, Ko'ichi presumably wanted to make some suggestions regarding the book I've agreed to write for their film about Marie Kuraki, the woman he mentions in his letter. The team he's with has been making videos for television until now, and this is to be their first full-length feature (Ko'ichi is in charge of recording).

The title is still undecided, but Ko'ichi wants to call it "Like a Mistress." Sergio Matsuno, the man backing the project, has a different idea. I, too, have something in mind for it, though I'd prefer not to reveal it at this early stage. "Like a Mistress" is definitely not bad. It just doesn't evoke the image I have of her, which is rather more complicated than anything suggested by "a mistress," since she seems to have put roots down inside me, roots that go uncomfortably deep.

The title Matsuno proposed when he came from Mexico to ask me to write the story of Marie's life, on which the film will be based, is absolutely inspired—what else can you say about "The Last Woman in the World"! I intend to record the talk I had with him in detail toward the end of this account; for the moment, though, I will simply try to show how serious the idea behind his outrageous-sounding title actually was.

Marie Kuraki spent the last few years of her life helping to run a cooperative farm in the Mexican countryside, devoting herself to the health of the Indians and mestizos who worked there. While she was there she came to be regarded as a saint, not only in the village where the farm was, with a pyramid—an Aztec ruin—looking down on it from a high mountain peak, but also in the neighboring villages from which some of these poor workers came. Of course, not actually having been there to confirm the story, I am merely passing on what I heard from Matsuno, the manager of the farm; yet nothing Ko'ichi, Asao, and the rest of the team, now there on location, have told me so far conflicts with his report.

Matsuno is planning to show Marie's movie on a sheet rigged up somewhere on the farm or in the main square of one of the villages in the area, whenever there's a festival or some such event. At first there will be other films as well, mainly ones directed by Kurosawa, but ultimately the film about Marie's life will become the only feature, shown over and over again.

While we were drinking at my house, Matsuno got into a maudlin mood and his talk took on a visionary quality. The end of the world was near, he said; he'd felt it in North America, too, but even more strongly here in Japan. "We are so poor in Mexico, there is nothing we can do to turn the tide.... As the end approaches, the people Marie loved so much, on the farm and in the village, will sit facing the steep mountain with the Aztec pyramid on top, their backs to the gravel desert that stretches out beyond their little plot of level land. They will have hung up a makeshift screen, and here they will spend the last days watching Marie's film. For these people, the close-up projected onto that broad white sheet as it flaps in the wind will be the image of 'the last woman in the world.' An actress will play Marie in the dramatic parts, but for the last scene we want to use a photograph, a still image that will stay there forever on the screen...."

This was said in the course of his visit to ask Asao and me for help with the movie, and to tell me about Marie's illness; and although I couldn't help smiling at the cosmic scale his conversation acquired when drink had loosened his tongue (which wasn't, after all, out of keeping with the gravity of the subject), I was deeply moved by it. I remembered the village of Malinalco, also at the foot of a mountain with an Aztec pyramid on top, which I had visited while I was in Mexico City some time ago, climbing to the summit, then making my way down the seemingly endless path to the valley below.

In the dream I had that night, some Mexicans were gazing up at a photograph of a Japanese woman, projected onto a sheet they had hung in the middle of a vast plain where black lizards scampered up twisted willow trunks. In Malinalco, there was a narrow belt, stretching from the pyramid on the mountain down to the valley, where nearly every variety of bush and tree in Mexico could be found. With this scrubby foliage in the background, in a world where everything was dying, the image of an emaciated Japanese woman in her mid-forties loomed over the lifeless desert. The sun came up behind the mountains, bleaching the screen white, but with the passing hours it sank below the horizon, and the photograph reappeared. No one rewound the reel, so the last scene lingered there, just as it was....

I, too, remember Marie as Ko'ichi spoke of her in his letter, working in Sukiyabashi Park. She appeared to me, from where I sat in the tent, as a figure bathed in bright sunlight, an image seen through an overly powerful lens. She would glide across in front of me, from right to left, her broad forehead, flat all the way to the hairline, in balance with the straight, well-shaped nose; the smile, intelligent, but with a wide-open look to it. The outline of this image, which I saw in profile, was stunningly clear, and the colors equally vivid, for I was deep in shadow, while she was outdoors in a shower of light.

Although I was only a few feet away, I never thought of offering to help when she was about to lift something heavy; I simply watched her slip by in front of me. In the tent, I was taking part in a hunger strike, and Marie was a volunteer giving us support. Concentrating on this memory a bit more, I can see three beaming young men in the sunshine, following Marie around as she cuts across the space in front of the tent.

That was ten years ago. Surrounded by various companions, I sat in the hunger strikers' tent, a miserable stubble on my face. The sickly trees outside mustered what greenery they could to wave in the June breeze....

A young Korean poet had been thrown in jail and sentenced to death for "violation of the Anti-Communist Law." A group of intellectuals sympathetic to the poet's political activities, who were still in contact with him, had organized this hunger strike to protest against the Korean government. In the tent were experts on the Korean situation, social historians, peace activists concerned with the human rights movement in Asia, and *zainichi* writers and poets, natives of Japan with Korean citizenship.

More than anything, it was the literary quality of the poet's work that had moved me to join them. In that sense, I was somewhat out of step with the others in the tent. I probably could have discussed the poetry of this man we were trying to save, although with doubtful chances of success, with Mr. Lee, the *zainichi* novelist sitting next to me, for I had first come to know it through his translations. But he was engrossed in a lively debate about the meaning of our political message and the action we were now taking. In an atmosphere like that, it would have been difficult to begin talking about the correlation between the Russian theorist Bakhtin, whose writing I was absorbed in at the time, and the system of images in this poet's work.

Outside the tent, younger activists were collecting signatures for a petition and calling for donations, as well as passing out pamphlets on Asian problems, written by intellectuals of the so-called "New Left." The pamphlets began with the question, asked both in anger and dismay, "Why have we no real writers like this Korean poet in Japan?" and then went on to analyze the current situation of the democracy movement in Korea. The constant refrain of the speeches outside which we could hear in the tent was, "Why should a poet be sentenced to death simply for writing poems?" A reasonable question, no doubt. I myself was participating in this hunger strike to protest against the dictatorship responsible for such acts, but as I listened to these young people, so sure of themselves as they repeated their slogans, I found myself thinking—yes, but isn't it more logical for a poet to be sentenced to death for writing poems than for doing anything else?

In the midst of this slogan-shouting, the presence of Marie, as she poked her head in from time to time to see how I was, and with great efficiency took care of whatever needed to be done outside, gave me a sense of intimate encouragement. She would swiftly stoop down and peer into the tent, catching my eye with that playful, wide-open look, on a face that also had the seriousness of a studious college girl. At moments like these I would feel I too had become one of the young men who followed her around, willing to do anything for her. It was a sweet, sentimental feeling, as though I were still a student with a beautiful older woman, a relative of mine, to watch over me.

But of course she was younger than I was, about thirty-six or -seven at the time. When I think of Marie as she was then, a word that immediately comes to mind is "wide-open," which I've already used several times. And yet there was great suffering in her home, which she had to bear the brunt of; you could read it in her eyes, always in shadow beneath the long lashes and perfectly straight eyebrows, which served to emphasize the impression of seriousness. She was too much on the move for any casual observer to have seen all that, though.... The other volunteers apparently saw her as a worker who had a natural, feminine radiance but didn't talk much.

I knew of the problems in Marie's home because that was how we had become acquainted. For her, the democracy movement in Korea and the poet who led it were not matters of much concern.

She had come out of consideration for my wife, who had a similar problem that kept her at home.

At the time, my older son was enrolled in the high school division of the Aotori School for the Handicapped, near Sangenjaya. When Marie's older child entered the junior high division, one of the teachers, seeing that their handicaps were similar and that they shared an interest in classical music, thought they might get along, and introduced them. The friendship between the boys naturally brought the mothers together as well. Once when my wife was unable to go to a concert of Bach's *St. John Passion*, to be directed by a German organist, I used the tickets she'd bought through the Mothers' Union and went with my son. Marie had brought her boy, too, and it was there that we met for the first time.

When they saw each other in the crowded, dimly lit lobby, the boys stood there calmly for a while, their faces grave yet full of warmth, and exchanged greetings in voices too low for me to hear. I realized that this was Musan, and that the woman standing next to him in a silk dress with a decorative belt that hung down over her hips must be Marie Kuraki. I could see it both in her appearance and in the constant motion, the small adjustments the mother of a handicapped child is continually making, even when she appears to be standing still at his side. Amidst all the noise and activity it seemed all the more evident—this was definitely the Marie I'd heard my wife talk about.

She smiled without looking directly at me, as though she wouldn't have minded being ignored altogether, and, without so much as a hello, was carried away by the crowd. Entrusting himself to his mother, who pulled him along by the hand, Musan looked back at my son all the while, although I had heard that his eyes, like Hikari's, were so bad they couldn't be corrected completely, even by lenses with complex prisms....

The concert was held in a cathedral on a hill in Ichigaya. Leaving our coats on one of the front pews, on the aisle to the left, my son and I went out into the drizzle that had begun to fall. It was some distance to the men's room, and we had to go through patches of complete darkness on the way. When we returned, Marie and Musan, who had apparently also been to the bathroom, were sitting in front of us. Parents of handicapped children make a point of choosing seats near an exit, knowing that the child may need to use the bathroom during the performance, that his movements are awkward, that he may do something unexpected. The shoulders of Musan's navy blue serge jacket, which looked rather smart next to his pudgy white neck, were covered in a fine spray of raindrops. Marie's head, held perfectly straight in front of me, with several moles on the back of the soft white neck, and unblemished earlobes the texture of hardened wax, made me feel guilty about staring at her.

Toward the end of the first part of the *St. John Passion*, both Hikari and Musan were fidgeting. As soon as the intermission began, I leaned over and asked Musan if he would like to go to the bathroom; the strength of a man was needed to push through the noisy, jostling crowd, all the more to guide two handicapped children through the drizzle and dark to the cathedral restrooms, which were smaller than those in a public hall. Marie, in her dress with a wide collar, turned in her seat—her elegance and the brilliance of her smile no less impressive than the soprano soloist's—and, although she hadn't yet spoken a word to me, encouraged Musan to go with me as naturally as if the four of us had come as a family. Proud to have been entrusted with a younger schoolmate, Hikari moved with far greater agility than he had before, and Musan eagerly followed him.

As it turned out, most of the audience at the cathedral that day had done work connected with Christian volunteer organizations and understood the problems of the handicapped, so our trip to the men's room went quite smoothly. When I returned Musan to

Marie, she merely smiled and nodded. But then she turned around and, letting her fragrant handkerchief skim across the program I was reading, reached up to dab at the raindrops on my hair; the natural thing to do, perhaps, after drying Musan off. When Marie turned next to Hikari, I took the large handkerchief from her with a grateful gesture. But before I had time to actually thank her the music began, and as soon as the second part was over, we hurriedly rose to take our children home, as they were liable to have seizures if they were kept up too late.... This is how Marie and I first became acquainted.

We didn't have a real conversation until about a month later. As the father of a mentally retarded child, and a writer, I had been asked by the principal of my son's school to speak to a study group on the education of handicapped children. My wife invited Marie along. Since my mother-in-law had come up to Tokyo for a visit, we were able to leave the children with her.

I learned in the taxi we took together that Marie was divorced and had two children; she was raising her retarded son Musan, while his younger brother Michio, a bright boy enrolled in a well-known private elementary school, was with his father. With her mother there to take care of Musan during the day, she was also able to teach at a women's college in Yokohama. But recently her mother had begun to show signs of senility and that worried her a bit, she said, and it showed in her eyes, in shadow beneath the long lashes, despite the cheerful smile on her face. My wife must have already found out about all this while they were working together at the school; Marie was repeating it for my benefit, by way of introducing herself.

When my lecture was over, we went to a coffee shop by the station nearest the Koto Ward Hall, which the study group was using for its meeting. The shop was divided into a small bakery where bread and sandwiches were sold, and an area with tables where coffee was served, separated by a few steps and a row of potted plants. The raised area we sat in was a broad, open space, cut off from the goings-on next door. So soon after speaking to a large group, my emotions were still off-balance, too exposed, and while we talked, I was in the process of shutting them back in, shrinking them down to size. In other words, I was chattering away and then suddenly clamming up, at irregular intervals.

Marie's mouth was outlined all the way to the edge in bright red lipstick, and during one of my silences, she had this to say on the subject:

"Old-time movies and things are a fad now, and some of my students are collecting pencil cases and notebooks with Betty Boop on them. Seems they've started calling me 'Betty' behind my back. I'm sure these girls have never seen a Betty Boop movie, though. Neither have I, for that matter."

Now that she mentioned it—as a joke, to cover slight embarrassment—those lips really did have a Betty Boop look to them, an effect emphasized by the stray wisps of hair around the well-shaped forehead and the way the eyes, dark in shadow only a moment before, now sparkled....

"It's only natural for Betty Boop to be old-time to college girls now," my wife said. "But unlike you, Marie, I'm sort of a contemporary of Betty's. My father worked in the movies, so I got to see some Betty Boop films during the war. That shows how much of an age gap there is between us."

"I grew up in the middle of a forest," I said, "so the first time I was in a real movie theater was when we went to the next town, after the war. I only knew Betty Boop from comic strips in old magazines. As a contemporary, that is."

"You mean you never saw a movie before that, during the war? Or was there some sort of makeshift theater? I'll probably be lumped together with Marie's students just for asking, though...."

"Well, we did see some educational films, on the second floor of the Farmers' Cooperative." Feeling lumped together in the same generation, my wife and Marie both laughed. "We used to sit on straw mats, with the bugs crawling up our knees."

I had been aware for some time now of three young women, standing near the vague boundary between the bakery and the coffee shop, each clutching a bag of bread. My lecture had been the morning session, and in the afternoon the meeting was to break up into small groups to hear reports from teachers in schools for the handicapped. Participants would naturally be having lunch in the area. Dressed in faded jeans, as though this was what they wore for both everyday and special occasions, all three were solidly built, their weight centered in their legs and hips. They exchanged nods and strode toward us.

"Er, may we talk to you for a minute?..." They lined up beside the little table, their muscular shoulders touching. Since there was no room to ask them to sit down, I stood up to hear what they had to say.

They were taking part in the meeting as teachers at a school for the handicapped in Tokyo. For the past two or three years—in other words, since these three young women had begun working there—the annual excursion for the high school division had been a trip from the Kansai area to Kyushu, including a visit to the Atomic Bomb Museum in Hiroshima. They considered this an important experience for both the students and the teachers and helpers who accompanied them. But in this year's schedule, it was to be replaced by a trip to Miyajima, a well-known scenic area. The principal and head teacher said the change had been made in answer to a request from parents of third-year students, and since more than half were in favor of it, they had no objection to it. Rather than go to Miyajima to see the deer, however, they themselves wanted to take their pupils to the Atomic Bomb Museum and show them things that had once belonged to schoolchildren who had been burned to death in the world's first

17

nuclear catastrophe. Until now, children who had been to the museum had clearly been changed by the experience....

Both the girl who was doing the talking and her two silent supporters were obviously well equipped to be teachers of the handicapped, mentally as well as physically, and had been putting their ability to good use. I was particularly drawn to the speaker, whose face showed such determination she almost looked fierce. The skin at the neckline and below the sleeves of her plain blouse was dry from too much exposure to the sun, and bore the mark of hard physical labor unusual for a young woman. She and her friends, their hips and thighs filling their jeans to capacity, exuded a sense of bulk, of sheer volume, but rather than being put off, Marie and my wife were enthralled. I could sense that clearly even as I stood there listening, looking down. My wife seemed overwhelmed by the vigor of these women, much younger than herself; while Marie, who was still a match for them, acknowledged this vigor with a wry smile....

In my lecture that morning, I had expressed various opinions as the father of a handicapped child. I had also written a book concerning the atomic bombing of Hiroshima. Knowing that these two issues were of great concern to me, the girls were hoping to get my support for their efforts to reinstate the trip to Hiroshima. But my immediate reaction was to imagine Hikari, dressed in his traveling clothes, standing in front of the display cases in the Atomic Bomb Museum. I could even see him listening in shock, trying to understand as T, the curator, an old friend of mine who had himself been exposed to radiation, explained how many thousands had died instantly, or lived on in agony....

"I suppose you'll just have to respect the will of the parents whose children are actually going on the trip, taking all the minority opinions into account, too," I finally managed to say.

Openly showing their disappointment, the girls eyed one another, still intent apparently on giving it one more try. And then Marie broke in, the smile gone from her Betty Boop face, replaced by a dark, troubled look:

"You say that seeing the Atomic Bomb Museum clearly changed the children, but I wonder in what way. They were able to travel, so I'm assuming they were above a certain level of intelligence. Surely you don't mean the horror of it all left them petrified—and therefore easier to control? My son gets in a panic at the very idea of death, so I'm sure it would leave him in despair—is that the kind of 'change' you're referring to? As a mother, I'd worry more about the shock he'd get ... that he'd never be able to forget it, and recover from it."

Listening to this comment, especially the last part, which Marie obviously made as much for her own sake as for theirs, my wife nodded, apparently also imagining Hikari in Hiroshima. The summer our boy was born with a deformity in his skull, before we knew whether or not he could be operated on—the doctor had not yet offered us any possibilities, and I was not ready to make a decision—I had briefly explained the situation to my wife, who was home from the hospital by then, and left at once for Hiroshima. I had been asked to write about an international conference on the banning of nuclear weapons, but the conference turned into a shambles, and in the meantime I went to visit the Atomic Bomb Hospital. From the doctors and patients I met there, I received the kind of encouragement that can only come from people who have lived through an immense tragedy. Only then was I able to move toward accepting the child in a positive way. And now I stood looking down at my wife, as she wondered how Hikari would recover once he had been "left in despair"....

"If you want to know how Hiroshima changed our students, we can show you the compositions they wrote afterward."

"Well, I can't say anything definite without actually reading them ... but even if a normal child were to go to Hiroshima and come back somehow transformed, that would be quite something, wouldn't it?"

"We believe that being handicapped can make children all the more sensitive to really important things."

"It's gratifying to know there're teachers who feel that way. So when they go to Hiroshima, dedicated people like you will be there to guide their reactions in the right direction, is that what you mean?"

"Without seeing for ourselves exactly how the children changed," I interrupted, "I don't see how we can judge this properly, Marie. So you think it's better not to show the effects of the atomic bomb directly to very young or handicapped children, do you?"

"A lot of mothers feel that way, but we'd like them to see things differently," the girls remarked.

"Well, that's certainly not the way *I* feel. The American woman writer I've been reading since I was a student, and am teaching now, says that everything that's happened in the world since the bombing of Hiroshima is related to it, and I couldn't agree more. I'm convinced that something went wrong with my baby because it was born into this world, after Hiroshima.... I shouldn't really be dragging myself into it like this, though."

"That's OK. We think so, too. And that's why we want to show the children what happened at Hiroshima."

"But aren't there lots of ugly, brutal, even devastating things going on at school, and in the children's homes? And aren't these the things that young teachers like you, and the children themselves, have to face every day, whether you like it or not? Once we've accepted the fact that this post-Hiroshima world is our reality, we've just got to pick ourselves up and keep on going. It's fine to take handicapped children to Hiroshima. It's important to actually see the horror of what happened there. If you can somehow make a connection between that and what goes on at school and in their homes—not as an 'idea' you've spoon-fed them, but on the level of their own everyday experience—then you'll really have achieved something. But if you're just feeling pleased with yourselves when you find traces of an 'idea' you've taught them in the compositions they write afterward, then I'd rather you didn't bother, at least with my child."

The girls seemed to have lost the will to go on arguing with Marie, or even to speak to me as I stood there in silence. They had all turned a deeper shade of red beneath their sunburn, and their faces looked puffy. They bowed and turned to leave, then made their way down the steps of the narrow passageway to the bakery, the hips of their jeans bulging out over thighs like pillars. Watching them retreat, my wife sighed and said:

"What wonderful teachers; just imagine how hard they work, and yet they put so much thought into it as well." I honestly agreed with her.

"You can say that again. That's the type I'd like for Musan's teacher," Marie added, watching them go with wide-open eyes, making me sympathize with a certain regret I saw there as well....

And so I became friends with Marie, who later came to the hunger strike in Sukiyabashi Park, not so much out of an interest in politics or human rights as to help me personally. Although they didn't go so far as to call for donations, or hang placards around their necks with petitions on them, Marie and her three young men kept themselves busy doing odd jobs like cleaning up the area or taking visitors' shoes from the front entrance of the tent to the exit at the back, lining them up so the owners could find them easily when they were ready to leave.

And once when she'd returned from a meal, she did something I'm unlikely to forget. She came right up to my side, which was unusual in itself, carrying a thermos jug. Taking a styrofoam cup from the stack she'd brought along with the thermos, she

21

poured out a drink for me. I took a sip, thinking it must be iced tea or something, and tasted honey and lemon, flavored with a complicated blend of spices—a drink as thick as molasses, and probably far more nutritious than your average solid food! Although there were no hard and fast rules among the participants, I had joined the strike determined not to take in anything but water, and as little of that as possible, so I was in two minds about drinking the rest. But S, sitting next to me, a specialist in the history of the Occupation and a man whose studies in America had given him a practical approach to things, whisked away the cup I'd set down by my knee and drained it, his Adam's apple bobbing up and down as he drank. He then blithely pronounced it absolutely wonderful, and so the thermos jug, along with the styrofoam cups, was passed up and down and back and forth, all around the tent.

That evening, Marie appeared once again, kneeling at the low entrance before coming in to collect the thermos. She gaily thrust her squarish chin toward the front of the tent. In the space outside, which I could see from where I sat, a big-boned older woman who resembled her stood smiling at me, holding a serene-looking Musan by the hand. Now that her work for us was finished for the day, Marie had met up with her mother, who had brought the boy along, and the three of them were probably on their way to a concert. The perfect calm on the boy's face and the dignified bearing of this elderly woman, when combined with the generosity Marie had shown us from the start, seemed to turn the hunger strike into something quite civilized, with plenty of breathing space, which pleased me a lot.

On the last night of the hunger strike, there was a violent rainstorm. Although we sensed that the roof was gradually getting lower and lower, our brains were sluggish, more from lack of sleep than hunger, so despite this ominous feeling, no one actually bothered to examine the roof, with one naked light bulb hanging

22

from it. That night, when I sat up to greet S, who had come back from the newspaper office where he'd gone to write an article, he lay down in the space I had vacated, so I lost my place to sleep. After a while, Mr. Ko, a *zainichi* poet, took pity on me, and I had just managed to squeeze myself into the crack beside him when the canvas above us bulged like a hernia in a rubber balloon, and anyone could see we were in trouble. Yet even as we lay there, cowering beneath the heavy rain, no one was able to do anything about it. But then three young men in plastic raincoats hesitantly entered the tent. Carefully, so as not to damage the canvas, they guided the huge puddle over the side of the tent. When they had finished pouring the water off, they set up a prop, thus saving us the trouble of watching the rain collect there again. The next morning, when I asked the leader of the young activists about the three who had apparently stayed there all night, guarding against further mishaps, he said: "Those guys came with that teacher from the women's university, but they've already left. They don't seem interested in joining the movement, but they sure worked hard last night."

That afternoon, the three-day hunger strike ended and we gathered by the tent, now being taken down, to discuss plans for a press conference. Marie was suddenly at my side, as though she'd slipped into place from out of nowhere. She was taking Musan and the three young men to spend a couple of nights at her summer house in Izukogen. Since there was nowhere to park, the youngsters were driving around the block while she dropped in to give me a shaving kit; I'd already looked pretty shabby the day before, apparently. So when I appeared clean-shaven at the press conference on the news that evening, among the haggard participants with their three-day beards, I alone looked fresh, and strangely out of place.

"It was like you'd been playing hooky during the hunger strike, hiding out somewhere, and then suddenly popped up for the press conference," my wife laughed. "But Marie thinks if you're going to get a bunch of people together to do something, it's silly not to have a good time while you're at it. Even if it's a hunger strike, you might as well be neat and clean when it's over."

The vehicle that appeared after driving once around the Ginza was a special sort of jeep, and the young men in it, transformed from hunger-strike helpers into carefree college boys again, looked ready for a party, preferably down by the beach, with water sports thrown in. The other helpers still taking down the tent, partners for a time in promoting a political and human rights message, had the same drawn faces and rumpled, dirty clothing as the rest of us. Marie hurried over to the jeep, her high heels clicking on the pavement, and the driver, without so much as a sympathetic backward glance, lifted her lightly into the passenger seat (I caught a glimpse of Musan's beaming face, off to one side), revved the engine, and drove away.

| 2 |

There was something undeniably refreshing about a beautiful woman in her thirties, divorced, working, and thoroughly enjoying life, despite having a handicapped child and mother to care for (actually, it seemed to be the old mother who made that life possible). The phrase "merry widow" came to mind. It was now autumn, the season for festivals and things of that sort, and my wife, getting tireder by the day, seemed to be struggling a bit when she left for our son's school to help prepare for the Mothers' Union Bazaar. As I saw her off, I found myself wondering if, under Marie's influence, she might not actually enjoy herself. But Marie's special view of the world and the way she had of expressing it, as demonstrated to the young teachers that day in the coffee shop, was to result in discord among the mothers.

One day shortly before the bazaar, when my wife was working all day at school, I went to pick Hikari up, and by the front gate exchanged greetings with Marie's mother, who had come to meet Musan. Far from appearing senile, she seemed to me an intelligent woman, her mind occupied with serious thoughts, but she was very pale, and I wondered if there was something wrong.

My wife came home late that night, absolutely exhausted, and in a rotten mood. She couldn't even muster the energy to go to the bedroom and take off her makeup without first airing her grievances about what had happened at school. When I had brought her a cup of tea at the kitchen table, she told me that an argument had broken out over something Marie had said, and although she sympathized with the anti-Marie faction, she didn't want to leave her friend completely on her own, and so had kept quiet (wearing herself out with the effort) as Marie, a bright smile on her heavily made-up face, stubbornly refused to give an inch.

A while before, a girl named Sanae, a student in the junior high school division, had suddenly died. Afflicted with both Down's syndrome and a heart defect, Sanae was nevertheless a remarkably attractive child who was always chosen to be the queen or princess in the school play, and never failed to delight both the people who put it on and the parents who came to watch. I had never spoken to her, but her sweet nature came across naturally, even to those of us who merely watched from the sidelines. When she died of a heart attack, everyone mourned; then, after a while, her class teacher suggested making a book about her, with pictures of her in school plays and on excursions, as well as short memoirs by classmates, teachers, and parents who had known her. There were also Sanae's own very simple compositions and diary, and the newspaper reporter who was helping them find a publisher—he had written an article about Sanae's death—assured them that the book would have plenty of appeal for the general market.

It was a plan everyone else enthusiastically supported, but Marie had been so set in her opposition to it that the women teachers, who were already at work on the project, finally broke down and even started crying. Consciously trying to suppress her own negative feelings and stay as neutral as possible, my wife told me what had happened.

"I liked Sanae, too," Marie had said; "she was a lovely, gentle child. She was openly affectionate toward me, just as she was with everyone. At the funeral, one of the teachers, Sister T, asked why such a beautiful child, a constant source of comfort and encouragement not only to her friends and family but to her teachers as well, had had to die so young. We should all try to understand why god has done this, she said, and everyone nodded earnestly. Yet if this was god's will, it was also his will that Sanae, so charming and sweet, be burdened with Down's syndrome.

"Shouldn't we have already been asking, 'Why has god done this?' at that stage? We all live with handicapped children. Each of us gets moral support from that particular kind of beauty, or charm, or gentleness that our child has. And yet each child is also marred by the inevitable ugliness that comes from being handicapped. And don't we see a warped, twisted quality in their hearts from time to time, too, that seems to go along with the physical deformity? The unsightliness we needn't even confirm for ourselves; the reactions of people who pass our children as they walk down the hill from school to the bus stop together serve as a mirror to show it to us, like an open sore. The other kind of ugliness we're forced to admit to ourselves. If we're going to work together to produce a book that tells the truth about handicapped children, I'd rather make it one that shows this warped, twisted quality. If we can't make society accept the whole truth, then that one book won't be worth all the bother it takes to put it together...."

"That blunt way of talking Marie has is usually so convincing," my wife went on, "but I'm afraid it rubbed me the wrong way today. And after she had us all stunned into silence, she got all the more defiant; it was as though she were challenging us.

27

And then she said: 'Sanae was lovely, kind, even had a sense of humor, and so we mourn her and want to commemorate her death. The whole idea behind this book makes me realize that something an American woman writer I've been reading since I was a student once said was absolutely right. Seeing handicapped children through a blurry film of sentimental tears, instead of facing the reality head on—all of it—reduces them to pathetic, cute little imbeciles; in the end, it leads straight to concentration camps, with smoke rising from the gas chambers....'

"When Marie said that, everyone gasped in horror. They were so wrought up they seemed ready to throw her out...."

"I think I know the American writer she was talking about," I said; "she developed an incurable disease when she was still quite young, but kept writing anyway. She was a devout Catholic, and an incredibly strong person besides. I don't imagine her way of thinking would strike much of a chord here in Japan, though, and if Marie was trying to force it down people's throats she'd meet with resistance anywhere, not just at the Mothers' Union in a school for the handicapped. Anyway, this writer says that kindness—'tenderness' is the word she uses—can lead to terrible things if it's cut off from its original source. When we hear people talking about 'poor handicapped children,' we feel they must be kind; yet among these same kindhearted people there've been some who went one step further and decided to isolate these children from the rest of society, to hide the poor things from staring crowds. And that leads to an institution.

"Something that's going to be a problem from now on is that women may be pressured into having abortions when some abnormality is discovered before birth. That's just the sort of thing those kindhearted people would want. I think that's what she means when she talks about kindness that's cut off from its source. And at the root of what she means by real 'tenderness' is god. There's a god, she says, who took on the human figure of Christ and, as a 'person,' redeemed the sins of mankind. Not being a believer myself, I can't say I understand completely, but then again maybe that's why it's stuck in my mind...."

"If Marie had explained herself in detail that way, she might have brought us around. We were all so angry—we couldn't see why our sympathy would lead to the gas chambers, but I think I see the point now...." Turning this over in her mind, my wife by now had lost any resentment she may have felt, and after a short pause she added: "I remember Marie once saying she didn't believe in Christianity, or anything else for that matter, but she's certainly done a lot of thinking about belief...."

The next disaster to befall Marie was of an entirely different kind from the squabble with the Mothers' Union. If left to run its course, it might even have developed into a scandal ripe for the weekly magazines. The photo tabloid *Focus* hadn't appeared yet, but Marie, with her striking looks and fashionable clothes, along with her determination to fight for what she believed in, would undoubtedly have been an ideal target for it. Her job being at a women's university, if the tabloids had managed to have their fun with her I'm sure she would have been forced to resign. So I did what I could to see that things didn't develop in that direction, thus repaying her for the support she'd given me during the hunger strike.

It was the three young men who had helped us in the tent in Sukiyabashi Park who told me about it. When one of them called to say they'd like to see me, I suggested they come over sometime that afternoon, but he replied that it wasn't the sort of thing they wanted to discuss in my study, and if we talked in the living room my family might overhear; they were afraid that would make me even more uncomfortable. The youth on the telephone was being extremely wary on my behalf. And so we decided that they would give me a ride to the pool where I went to swim five or six times a week at the time, and we would talk about it in the jeep on the way.

We met outside the house and started off, with me in front on the passenger's side, Asao, who had made the telephone call, driving, and the other two in the back; but unable to hide their disgust for what they now had to tell me, all three sat in silence, their tanned faces set in a sullen pout. Having grown up when private cars were a rarity, I couldn't help babbling on about how much I appreciated the ride. Like "the man at table who has no sooner washed his hands than he begins to speak" (to borrow a phrase used by the ancient Greeks to show their contempt for someone they considered uncouth), I brought up one topic after another, and ended up feeling quite put out by their refusal to speak.

But when Asao, gathering courage from the fact that because he was driving he didn't have to look me in the face, finally started to tell me why they'd wanted to meet me, I realized that they were furious about the sheer vulgarity of something that had happened, and were hoping I would know how to deal with it.

From around the time of the hunger strike, the three of them had been acting as personal bodyguards for Marie, and when she was free they would do things together, sometimes taking Musan along, sometimes not. Several times she had invited them to the summer house in the hills of Izu that had belonged to her father, who had been a retired company executive, and this winter they had even gone skiing three or four times, with Marie, who was very athletic, acting as a coach.

There was a cafe-bar in Harajuku that Marie and the trio of young men used as a base—such places had just begun to appear in Tokyo, and weren't as popular then as they've since become. One day when the three of them were there with her, Marie had met a recording engineer who worked for a television station. Later, she apparently started seeing him from time to time with-

30

out them. Since they were bodyguards, "untainted by carnal love," and Marie was a grown woman who had once been married, they didn't interfere in that aspect of her life. But before long she seemed to be avoiding the man from the television station, and they felt the inevitable had happened.

This is where the story actually begins, with Marie subdued, not at all herself, and her young friends occasionally hearing her moan, "Oh god, I can't take it any more!" Figuring it was something to do with the TV engineer, they had asked her about it, just when Marie herself had made up her mind to tell them everything, in detail. She had slept with him several times, she said, but when she stopped answering his calls, he started threatening her. Putting his technical skill to use, the man had rigged up a hidden microphone (in the course of the relationship she had gone to his apartment—only once, though she now admitted it had been a mistake) and recorded them in bed. If Marie insisted on cutting off the relationship unilaterally, he would send the tape to the dean of the college where she worked, and he had plenty of copies ready to circulate among the parents of her students. The original was already in Marie's mailbox.

If I happened to know someone at the television company, they suggested, couldn't I have him talk to the lovesick recording engineer and make him stop this bullshit? Assuming, of course, that in this day and age there were still people in television with enough company loyalty to listen to the advice of an older employee....

Anyway, I promised them I would talk to Marie myself. I would meet her at the sports club, where I'd be going the next day at around the same time; I would be waiting near the reception desk, and we could talk in the lobby there.

Once it was all settled, the dour expressions of a moment before vanished, and Asao and company, now all laughter and high spirits, let me out in front of the club and drove off. Watch-

31

ing the wine-colored jeep fade from sight, I found myself once again noting in admiration the way the three were dressed, in a style that was conservative yet distinctive. When I was a student, most of us dressed passively, almost accidentally. Young people today, however, while seeming determined not to assert themselves in almost every other way, obviously choose their clothes with a careful sense of their own style. That this impressed me so deeply at the time showed how out of touch I was, and now that I thought of it, I realized it had been quite a while since I'd had any contact with the new generation more lasting than the present brief encounter.

The next day, having left the house in such a rush that my wife teased me about it, I reached the reception desk earlier than the time I had vaguely suggested, and when I took a look around, there was no sign of Marie among the young mothers who had brought their children for swimming or dance lessons. I showed my member's card at the desk, and asked the attendant if someone by her name was looking for me. He was a part-time employee, a physical education major with muscles so overdeveloped he looked like Tarzan; his mind, however, was apparently an entirely different matter, for he always spoke with the same mechanical politeness. He now answered, with a certain expression that told me Marie had ignored the club rules and marched right in: "You'll find her waiting in the members' lobby, sir."

I saw her immediately from the bottom of the stairs, her sunflower print skirt spread out around her, calmly sitting with legs crossed and head held high, looking straight ahead. Her straw hat, narrow-brimmed like a soldier's headgear, was held against her chest, and she waved it at me, looking as though she belonged in some summer resort. That cheery image was oddly at variance with her air of embarrassment, mixed with an "oh-what-the-hell" attitude clearly intended to give herself courage; years later, when my younger son came home and reported that he had failed his university entrance exam, the expression on his face would remind me of Marie that day....

"Oh, so you brought your swimming things, too? I'll go and buy you a guest member's ticket," I said, looking down at her, seeing the plastic carryall with her swimsuit in it on the floor by her knee.

"I guess I should have had something like that to get in here, too," Marie promptly replied. "When he saw me taking my shoes off, the boy at the desk didn't know what to do."

After I had handed her guest's card in at the front desk, I came back to find Marie, her face now looking quite composed, smoking a cigarette, those shadowed eyes trained on some far-off place. I explained where the women's locker room was on the way down to the pool, and about the sauna where she could warm up in lieu of exercising before swimming. As soon as I was finished, she seemed ready to jump up and go and get changed.

"I've heard about that business from Asao. What shall we do?" I asked, prompting her to remember why she'd come.

"The tape, you mean? Here it is." The cassette, edged in white paper, unlike either blank tapes or the prerecorded kind with labels that they sell in record shops, clicked in its case as Marie took it from her handbag.

"And is this the only—how shall I put it—the only material evidence the other party has? Is there anything else? Letters, or photographs...."

"I wouldn't write to a stingy bastard like that, and you don't really think I'd pose in front of a camera with a time switch, do you?"

"You've listened to it, haven't you?"

"What? Why would I need to!? I know what's on it, me moaning and saying some dirty words, with him egging me on all the time—that's all!"

I put the tape in my locker along with my other things,

changed into my swimming trunks, and was waiting when Marie emerged. In accordance with club rules, she had taken off all her makeup, including the thick layer of lipstick, and, her face now like a gentle-looking boy, she strode toward me in a blue racing suit with white stripes. Her body was lithe and slim yet well-rounded, and as we walked down the steps, shoulder to shoulder, and sweated in the sauna, side by side, I noted with some surprise that there were also hard knots of muscle on her shoulders and upper arms.

"When I was in high school in America, they had me doing track and field, and my muscles haven't changed much since then." In the middle of a stretching exercise, her back bent double, Marie's voice sounded slow and easy as she spoke to me from between her thighs, lined up like two spindles below her firm hips.

But although she certainly had the attitude of an experienced athlete, with shining beads of sweat standing out on her skin and her thick black hair covered by a bathing cap that left the back of her neck and ears showing, giving her a freshness more reminiscent of Olive Oil than Betty Boop, she was oddly slow and awkward on the spiral staircase that led down to the pool from the dry room. She had taken out her contact lenses, she explained, and I felt, for the first time, that I'd caught a glimpse of the university lecturer, a specialist in a certain American woman writer.

Marie was a marvelous swimmer. When I told her I swam a thousand meters of crawl a day, she said: "Then I'll go first so I don't get too far behind; if I'm too slow, could you just poke me on the bottom of the foot?" But even though I was trying hard, by the time I had crossed the pool three times I was so far behind that Marie, who had already made the turn and was on her way back, passed me in the middle of the pool. As she sped by, my own tendency to sink gave me the feeling of being on the bottom looking up, watching her perfectly straight body and vigorously

34

kicking thighs skim along the surface. Seeing that the first five hundred meters of trying to keep up with her had thoroughly exhausted me, she did a quick turn, swam another two hundred at top speed, and then climbed out of the pool, scarcely out of breath.

Marie disappeared into the locker room and took her time there, as though that were the only place where she would be slower than me. I slipped the tape she'd handed me earlier into the Walkman that I used to listen to foreign language tapes in the train on the way to and from the pool, and put the earphones in my ears … not without the feeling that I was doing something shameful in front of the other members relaxing in the lobby.

I heard the sporadic conversation of a man and a woman, reproduced in a quality of sound fine enough to pick up even the slightest crinkling of the sheets, belying any preconceptions I might have had about recordings done by hidden microphones. They soon switched to sex, and then back to conversation. When they were about to have sex again, with the composure of an older woman toward a younger man, the female voice said: "Let's do it from behind this time," followed by a rustling of sheets, and then "Wait a minute, I'll spread my legs." The man, who had meekly followed instructions at first, seemed to gain confidence after seeing the woman go wild in the throes of orgasm, and said: "I came twice, and look at this." To which the woman replied, in a husky voice that obviously came straight from the heart: "You're huge. Twenty-three—that's youth for you."

The man was a combination of youthful egotism and the passivity that comes from inexperience, but as they repeated the act, he gradually grew bolder. This natural change in him interested me, but I also noticed a shift in the woman's attitude; in the beginning she took the lead, assuring the man that she was on the pill before they had sex, calming him with her experience, but after the second time, she yielded to him, allowing herself to be the

35

gentle, malleable one. This, I felt, showed a certain kindness, and I liked her for it. And yet though the recording was technically well made, I couldn't make a connection between the woman's voice on the tape and Marie. It definitely had something of Marie's "wide-open" quality and good nature, but the voice was in no sense that of a woman who had undergone any kind of intellectual training.

"You're listening to that here? You dirty old man!" Brimming with life after physical exercise, her jet-black hair, still wet, brushed out around her head, and her lips once again bright red à la Betty Boop, Marie suddenly appeared at my side.

Taken by surprise, I felt my heart pound in my chest, but by that time I was convinced that it wasn't Marie's voice I was listening to on the tape.

"Like to hear a little?"

"Who, me? Hell no."

"I think this is a 'peeper's tape' he must have bought somewhere. Maybe at a porn shop where they sell 'Sex Toys'...."

"I have lots of different voices, you know, depending on the time and situation."

Leaving the tape running, I placed the Walkman and the earphones neatly in front of her and went to the vending machine in the corner of the lobby to buy us some beer.

"I can't believe this woman! She sounds so stupid; I mean, her heart's in the right place, but what a dumb broad!" she said, laughing.

I laughed as well to show her I agreed. It seemed to me that the problem was already half solved. Being a recording engineer, the young man from the television station must have dreamed of taping himself and his older lover in bed. But his fear of her catching him at it must have been just as strong. When Marie refused to see him any more, he was no doubt seething with thoughts of revenge, and wished he had made the recording after

36

all. And then he'd found this 'peeper's tape,' with the voices of an older woman and her young lover ("Twenty-three—that's youth for you"). It must have been his longing for a sweet, romantic fantasy he had built around Marie that drove him to this shoddy attempt at blackmail, with the bottom about to fall out of it any minute; I simply couldn't see anything more complicated behind it than that.

I suggested that we send Asao and his friends to see the man in question and have them say, "All right, we've heard the tape but it has absolutely nothing to do with Marie, so trying to blackmail her with it won't get you anywhere, but if you continue this kind of harassment anyway, we'll register an official complaint through someone we know at your company." And in fact, after that, the man never bothered Marie again.

In the subsequent conversation I had with Marie while we drank beer in the lobby, we touched on other things that are far more clearly etched in my memory. The problem we'd started with was so bizarre that, along with the effect of the beer, it drew us out, and we ended up telling each other some of our innermost thoughts. But it was Marie who talked most.

First, about the American writer she was studying. With the caution and reserve that literary scholars often show toward writers, she had never actually mentioned the name of the author she specialized in, but when I asked her if the things she'd said that caused so much trouble with the Mothers' Union that day weren't based on her literary research, she took the initiative and began to talk.

"I thought about it afterward, and now I think I know why I made everyone so angry. There I was, talking away, and now I'm not sure how well I understood the passage I was basing my argument on. Anyway, I was in a really bitchy mood after that, and went to the next meeting late, but when I got there everyone acted as though nothing had happened. Your wife must have explained it all to them, along the lines of what she'd heard from you. And that's how I knew you'd read Flannery O'Connor.

"In connection with Musan, what I find most convincing in O'Connor's writing is what she says about sentimentality. There's a lot that's innocent about Musan. I'm sure the same is true of Hikari. Sanae, the girl who died, was quite the little lady sometimes, but always within the bounds of what was natural for her age, so we'd have to say that she was an innocent child, too. But don't you think that parents of handicapped children tend to overemphasize their children's innocence, perhaps without even realizing it? It's not the kids' fault; the responsibility lies with us, the parents. I like your novels with the character modeled on Hikari, but I think there's an emphasis on innocence there, too. When I say 'emphasis,' of course I don't necessarily mean that you go to the extremes that O'Connor herself does, though.... Don't you think we somehow cling to, even depend on, the innocence in our kind of children?

"O'Connor says that when innocence is overemphasized, it tends to become its exact opposite. But of course we've all lost it, from the start. According to her, we return to innocence through the redemption of Christ, not all at once, but slowly, over a long period of time. When this long process is skipped over in real life, we too quickly, too easily, reach a state of mock innocence, and that's what she calls sentimentality.... And that's what I hate more than anything. If I use that as an excuse for doing a lot of *un*-innocent things in real life, though, it's just my way of saying 'Piss off' to the rest of the world."

"Did you notice the change in the woman on the tape we were just listening to?" I asked. "The way she seemed to be teaching the boy at first—talking down to him—and then gradually a more kindhearted side of her came through? A sexual relationship is a process in real life, too; they took a long time at it, and gradually the woman seemed to come closer to innocence."

38

"You said you knew right away the woman on the tape wasn't me—was that because her voice was so much more innocent than mine?... O'Connor, incidentally, wrote what I was just telling you about now in a passage about the relationship between sentimentality and obscenity."

Encouraged by the beer, another thought occurred to me. The woman on the tape was definitely not Marie, but despite differences in the way that age and level of education came through in the voice and way of talking, it seemed quite possible that the young man sensed, in that impression of innocence, something that recalled the warmth and longing he'd felt for Marie while they were having sex. So in sending the "peeper's tape"—an attempt at extortion that was never expected to work, as he couldn't have foreseen that Marie would believe it was the real thing without even bothering to listen to it—he may have been trying to plead with her like an angry, frustrated child, saying "How can you leave me when you've found, through sex with me, this tenderness, this innocent way of enjoying yourself?"

But instead of telling her this, I asked: "Marie, are you a Catholic?"

"Me? Of course not! I want to be free to enjoy my sins, and that's exactly what I'm doing!" she said, her honey-colored irises, wreathed by the long eyelashes, gleaming with what looked like a smile, the anger in her expression rebelling against it. "Just because O'Connor is a Catholic writer, I don't think that means her readers have to be Catholic in order to understand her work. Didn't O'Connor herself say she was determined to transcend the hostility of non-Catholic readers, to give her works enough inner power to stand on their own?" But Marie soon calmed down, generously granted me permission to buy us more beer, and began talking about her home situation. "My mother's in pretty bad shape these days, so she can't take Musan to and from school while I'm teaching.... I haven't been sending him to school for a while now. If the Mothers' Union found out I'd got tangled up in a mess like this while I was keeping Musan at home, they'd tar and feather me. I'm really glad your wife knows how to keep a secret."

"So your mother's at home with Musan now?" I asked, checking the club's overly elaborate wall clock, and seeing that it was already past seven.

"My ex has every other Saturday off, so he'll be there with Musan's little brother Michio for the night. Just when my mother can't get around so well, my ex's second marriage goes on the rocks, so he's free to bring Michio over to see Musan. One of the benefits of misfortune, I guess."

This business with the tape had given me an opportunity to hear the background of Marie's current situation from my wife, who didn't normally go into much detail about the other mothers at our son's school. Marie had married a classmate while both were still undergraduates, majoring in English literature, apparently with the financial support of the Kuraki family, who had their own company. Marie went on to graduate school; her husband, who had failed the same entrance exam, got a job preparing foreign language materials for a textbook company. She had her first child, Musan, while still in the master's course, and went back to school after Michio was born. When Michio's mental development outstripped Musan's, they had been forced to admit that their older son was handicapped.

It would be hard to imagine anyone but Marie deciding to do what she did next. My wife had said: "Marie's husband doesn't say much, and it seems her whole family treated her like a princess, always let her have her own way. To indulge a child that way is one thing, but they kept it up even after she was married!" Marie divorced her husband, leaving Michio with him and taking Musan to raise herself. She told my wife that she thought Musan's birth might lead her to some kind of "atonement," and that she felt the joy she'd find as she moved toward it was meant for her alone. There was no need, she said, to drag her husband and their other, healthy son into a life dedicated to "atonement."

Although Marie's wishes weren't respected immediately, the divorce went through without much emotional upheaval, and life with the new family of her mother and Musan began. She finished her doctorate, and after they had spent some time together in America, while Marie was studying at a college in the Midwest, she had been hired by the women's college where she now worked. It seemed, though, that the family was actually living on the income from dividends on shares of their company's stock. And so the years had passed.

"Of course my mother was there, too, but I was young then, and all set to raise Musan on my own, no matter what. I thought I could give him the support he needed all by myself—both for his handicap and for the genuine, human side of him underneath. And behind it all, I think, was the feeling that I wanted us to be linked in a special relationship. As though no one, not my husband or even Musan's little brother, could come between us.... But I realize now that the life I started, based on this idea of mine, has only kept on going because I've had my mother's help.

"And now, when I do have to take care of Musan by myself, and honestly, it's no picnic, my ex-husband hits a dead end in his second marriage and suggests that we all get back together again. When he brings Michio over every other Saturday he does all sorts of things around the house, and especially on days like today he's a lifesaver. So even though I started out wanting to prove that I could do everything on my own, and bring Musan up too—and until now I really thought I'd managed to pull it off—I have to face the fact that I've always had support from the people around me."

"My wife said it would be nice if Musan and Michio could live together, since they get along so well. Also that you'd said there was no ill feeling that caused you to separate; it seemed divorce was what you'd finally arrived at as a way of taking full responsibility for Musan.... And that you yourself had said you sometimes feel it was a strange decision to have made in the first place...."

"If I do get back together with him, at least I won't have to bother with men from TV stations taping me in bed," Marie replied, a little drunk from the beer, and looking like Betty Boop in a scene from an early film where she was about to be attacked by an old derelict, with an expression that didn't match those striking features.

3

I didn't go into much detail about the tape when I talked to my wife that night; I just mentioned it as an amusing episode, and went on to assure her that things seemed to be headed in the right direction, with Marie and her former husband soon to be back together. But my wife didn't seem at all convinced.

"Marie was determined to raise Musan by herself and set the man free, even if she did need her mother's help to do it. That's the way she is.... Then her ex-husband and his second wife split up, so she thinks, now there's something I can do for him. She's just using her mother's illness as an excuse.... I can't help thinking she's putting herself out too much."

"But it seems to me it would at least be good for Musan to have her ex and the other, normal brother living with them."

"Didn't Marie tell you about Michio?... That's what I mean when I say 'that's the way she is.' There was an accident while her husband was still with his second wife, and now Michio's in a wheelchair. But of course she wouldn't mention that, not even to you. I think she's planning to haul her husband out of this crisis by plunging headlong into it herself, taking the whole burden, the two handicapped kids and all, on her own shoulders."

The gruesome tragedy that would occur in Marie's family a year later was reported in newspapers and magazines, even on television. If I try to reconstruct the incident myself from the information in these reports, the part where I have to talk about Marie's state of mind will inevitably be colored by my own preconceptions. At the same time, I don't believe it's possible for an outsider to see into the mind of a mother who has gone through an experience of that kind. So, rather than attempting to give an objective account of it, I'll leave the task of telling the story to the letters I received from her unfortunate husband who, having once resumed his life with Marie, was now utterly alone.

I don't think you'd call it "déjà vu," although being an amateur in such matters I can't say for sure, but I feel as though Michio's first accident was a scene I'd witnessed, from beginning to end, sometime in the past. I have never made much of an effort to communicate my inner feelings to the people around me (I know it would be presumptuous even to begin comparing myself to a writer like yourself), either when I was a student or after I started working in the textbook business. But after the accident, it was as though something hard, like a layer of plaque, had been scraped away from the core of my emotions (which were there after all, hiding inside me).

This is the scene that was so vivid in my mind, one I already knew well. A child, no bigger than a bean, is about to get on a bus. He peers inside, checks behind him and, relieved, climbs aboard. Just then, with a sneer like Nearsighted Magoo (the old man in the TV cartoon), a junior high school boy hiding in the seat behind the driver sticks his head out. The child leaps back, takes off as soon as his foot hits the ground, and is hit by a truck moving around the bus....

44

There was a reason those Nearsighted Magoo eyes were as vivid as if I were seeing them in a daydream. After the accident, at that same bus stop, I spotted the boy who'd been picking on Michio for months, refusing to leave him alone. Ignorance might be considered an excuse, but still I'd done nothing to stop him, and since all he had done was stick his head out from the shadow of a seat, I didn't hold him responsible. When he saw me at the bus stop that day, he must have known there would be no inquiry into his role in the accident, or the long months of torment he had given Michio, because he leered at me with a Nearsighted Magoo face that sent chills down my spine.

Michio's back was hurt, but from the waist up there wasn't a scratch on him. His legs didn't seem to be broken, either, and there were no cuts or gashes that I could see. Not a drop of blood anywhere. When I got to the clinic where he'd been taken and saw him lying there on a bed, the first thing I asked the doctor was if there was any brain damage. When he assured me that, although an EEG would be necessary, there didn't seem to have been a blow to the head, I informed Marie immediately, before contacting my second wife, with whom I was living at the time.

But while he was at the clinic, it became clear that Michio was not going to recover the use of his legs. He was moved to a university hospital, where they put him through a battery of tests, and there, before being sent home for therapy, he was told about the permanent change in his body. At first he seemed indifferent to the fact that paralysis was a burden he would have to live with for the rest of his life. It wasn't just that he no longer cracked jokes or clowned around in the way he had before (he was a clever lad, who had always enjoyed making people laugh). He seemed to have the attitude of someone watching an actor play his role on a stage—it was this actor who was now paralyzed from the waist down and would have to learn a new way of doing things. He was very quiet, strangely calm. Almost oblivi-

ous to me, he showed no emotion even when Marie and Musan came to see him.

Compared to the change that would come later, Michio seemed to accept his condition at the time. He told us things he had never mentioned before, about how he had been singled out for abuse by the older boy who rode to school on the same bus, and how one morning he had gone to school hours early to avoid him, and his homeroom teacher had seen him standing on the playground with his arms folded, gazing up at a tulip tree. By the time he went back to school, he said, that junior high kid would have graduated and gone away, so there'd be no need to worry about the bus stop any more; yet by that stage he had already begun practicing with the wheelchair we had bought him, which means he must have realized that this was how he'd be going to school when he went back, the bus being out of the question now....

Nevertheless, when the time came for Michio to start rehabilitation in earnest, training the muscles he could still control with the help of a therapist, he suddenly insisted that the paralysis was only temporary, and since one day he would get up and walk, there was no sense in learning how to use a wheelchair. The therapist told him bluntly he was paralyzed for life, and that he'd have to start by accepting it, and getting used to it; but this was too hard for a boy that age to take, and Michio spent several days buried under the covers, refusing to speak, especially to the woman who was my wife then. They'd never got along, but things were a lot worse between them now. I won't say anything more about her, but sometimes when I'd had a long meeting at work and was late getting home, I would hear muffled sobs coming from Michio's room.

That summer, Marie suggested we bring the boys together again, it had been such a long time, so I took Michio to the Kurakis' summer house in Izukogen, where she and Musan were

46

*waiting for us. The Kuraki family owned a construction com-
pany, and Marie's mother had had the house remodeled so that
Michio would be able to get around easily, and use the toilet, in
his wheelchair. Since the accident he had been depressed and irritable, but in Izu, where he had greater freedom of movement and
was reunited with his mother and brother, he seemed like his old
self again, clowning around in a way we hadn't seen for quite a
while.*

*We used to climb halfway up the grassy slopes of Hageyama,
"Bald Mountain," which was so conspicuous among the other
shrub-covered mountains that Michio said it must have been
designed as a practical joke. We would walk through the arbutus
trees, along a row of summer villas, and then, though it was a
struggle pushing the wheelchair, descend through a grove of oaks,
camellias, and himeyuzuriha, their roots crawling over the thin
layer of earth with rocks showing through underneath, and on
down to the huge boulders that lined the shore. Michio seemed
especially fond of the trail that followed the jagged shoreline,
with all its ins and outs, toward Jogasaki.*

*As far as physical development went, Musan was above av-
erage for a child his age, so he, too, was able to push Michio's
wheelchair on gentle slopes where the road was paved. He was
obviously proud to be helping his little brother this way. The
trail, along the top of a sheer cliff, had been made when this part
of the coast was first developed, but apparently no work had been
done on it since, so although the flagstones were carefully placed,
it was really rather dangerous. There would be sudden bends
with no protective railings and the waves sucking at the rocks
directly below.*

*That's partly why I suggested going to the beach instead, but
Michio wouldn't hear of it; I could understand his not wanting
to wear swimming trunks, sensitive as he was about his withered
legs, but he refused even to consider going down to that gentle*

47

stretch of sand beside the ocean. Even so, on the whole Michio had a good time in Izu, and Musan, knowing that his brother was way ahead of him in brain power, was delighted to find he could use his physical strength to help him.

It was this trip to the hills of Izu that set the stage for the later tragedy, but I mustn't get ahead of myself. I returned to Tokyo to find that my wife had left me. Michio stayed with me for a while, and then we moved back into the house where Marie was still living with Musan.

On our first evening together, while we were having dinner, my mother-in-law asked: "Michio, how are your legs?" Her words were filled with love and encouragement, but it was a pointless question, which Michio met with undisguised contempt. First of all, he reported coldly, taking government regulations and commuting problems into account, his choice of junior high schools, which would determine his future, had been reduced to zero. Displaying a newfound hatred for the boy who'd bullied him, whom he had scarcely mentioned up to now, he declared it was his intention to study law at university, pass the bar exam, and then track the bastard down. When Marie pointed out, "But won't the statute of limitations have run out by then?" he took the jackknife his grandmother had given him (it had been her husband's, a souvenir from America) and threw it at her, aiming so close that it skimmed her ear, though fortunately the blade was folded in.

Soon after this happened, Marie's mother passed away; it still makes me sad to think she died worrying about her two grandsons. Then, in the summer of the year after the four of us got back together, something infinitely worse happened—the thing you know about from the newspapers and television. It was during the first week of school vacation. I didn't need to go in to the office that day, and when I got up late, having drunk too much the night before, Marie was in a panic—Musan, Michio, and the

48

wheelchair were gone. She had already circled the house several times looking for them, and although it was quite chilly she was sweating, with wisps of hair plastered to her pale forehead, and her lips showing oddly white.

A while before, we had begun letting Musan push Michio around the block, on the condition that he didn't cross the intersection. Marie usually went with them, but Michio knew just how to guide Musan, and was better at talking to him and getting him to respond smoothly than anyone in the family.

Once when Marie wasn't with them, Musan had had a mild epilectic fit. "All of a sudden Musan just stopped and got real quiet," Michio told us. "I thought if he falls down we're in for it; honest, I was really scared. And then I realized he was actually using the chair to prop himself up, pressing down on the handles and edging it forward bit by bit. I waited that way for a while, and when Musan seemed to be all right again I said 'OK, let's go home now,' and he said, 'Sorry to keep you waiting!' On the way back he was even more careful than before, keeping right to the side of the road the whole time."

While we were searching the neighborhood, Marie told me that she'd noticed Michio was always at Musan's side recently, apparently talking to him about something important, but when she asked him what it was about, he just clammed up. The past two or three days, not wanting to hear whatever it was, Musan had even put his fingers in his ears to shut it out. This would make Michio furious, but it didn't stop him; his face flushed with anger, he went on talking to his brother with a dogged patience that was unusual for him, until, noticing Marie watching them, he abruptly fell silent.

And there was more. At one of his weekly rehabilitation sessions, he had been bawled out for not trying. The young therapist had obviously meant to be encouraging, but he came down hard on the boy, hammering away at the same message: since he was handicapped for life, he would have to find the courage to accept it, and deal with it. More shocked than angry, Michio had seemed depressed all the way home from the hospital....

Once I actually started listening to Marie, who was frantic by now, I realized for the first time how these things had been building up until they were more than she could handle. In other words, since we'd got back together again, I had continued to leave everything, even important matters like this, entirely up to her.

When we had thoroughly covered the vicinity of the house, I began to comb the area on my bicycle, in gradually widening circles (it's strange we hadn't thought of this before). Marie rushed off to the police. They had no information to speak of yet, but when she asked at the nearest train station, just to make sure, the attendant casually replied that he had seen Musan and Michio pass through early that morning.

This wouldn't be the first time Michio had gone somewhere by train without us, but before there had always been young student volunteers to ask passersby for help carrying the wheelchair up and down the stairs. Michio, so withdrawn since the accident, had apparently been outgoing enough that morning to charm perfect strangers into lending Musan a hand with the wheelchair, and they had put him on board without further ado. By that time, he'd already bought two tickets at the long-distance window to Izukogen Station, with a change at Odawara.

Using the pay phone in the station, Marie contacted the caretakers of the summer villa: if her boys turned up, would they please stop them from going anywhere, and keep an eye on them until she could get there? I was just passing the station on my bicycle when she ran down the steps to the street. She was ready to call the Izukogen police as well, and have them take a boy in a wheelchair and his retarded older brother into protective custody. But like a fool I stopped her. "If a child who can't walk has his brother push his wheelchair, and they go back to the place where they had fun together during summer vacation, so what?—that's not against the law, you know. And what would the police do with them anyway, even if they did find them?" This is what I said, but the image haunting me was of Michio in a closed room at the police station with a bunch of cops poking fun at him, hurting his pride, and Musan, beside himself, sensing they were in trouble but unable to grasp the situation, his confusion attracting more of the same abuse.

Just in case Michio tried to call us, Marie and I asked the young housewife next door to stay in the house, and headed for Odawara, where we would catch the express for Izukogen. But by the time we reached the station and checked at the nearest police box for news of the boys, it was all over. We were driven in a waiting patrol car to the police station in Ito, where the bodies of our two children had been taken.

At the police station we heard the eyewitness reports, from which I'll piece together an account of what happened. The boys took a taxi from the station to the place where the paved walk among the summer villas ends, and from there they entered the grove of oak and camellia trees. They found some obliging students who hoisted the wheelchair onto the narrow path through the woods and then pushed it over the roots and other obstacles to the flagstone trail along the cliff by the sea. Michio was an easygoing, likable boy before the accident; his engaging smile and manner must have been effective in recruiting volunteers.

The students had even promised to come back an hour later and give them a hand. With Musan positioned behind him again, Michio had seemed to be waiting for them to go away before setting off. But when he gave his brother the signal to start pushing, the boys—surrounded by camellias, himeyuzuriha, and huge oak trees—were not as alone as they thought they were.

As I've said before, that area of the coast is rough and jagged, *lined with sharp outcrops connected like the teeth of a huge saw. The early morning anglers had already left, but in their place atop the next ridge was a group of sightseers, who spotted a wheelchair making its way down the trail, visible in patches through the covering of trees. From where they were you can see a bend in the trail where the earth has crumbled away, leaving the craggy surface of the cliff exposed, all the way down to the breakers. Realizing how dangerous it was, the group gathered at the edge, yelling and gesturing to the two boys to stop.*

The sound of the waves muffled their voices, but the boy in the wheelchair had reacted, lifting his head, apparently straining to hear. Suddenly, the wheelchair ground to a halt; he must have put on the brake.

Clumsily, but with great determination, the one who had been pushing, and who had bumped against the backrest when the wheelchair stopped, struggled to force it on down the trail. Then, giving up, he slipped past it and walked calmly forward. The cries of warning from the ridge were redoubled, with the boy in the chair apparently joining in, calling from behind.

As if to shut out all these voices, the boy put his fingers in his ears and kept on going, his elbows sticking out, until one foot was hanging in the air ... and he followed it over the cliff. There was a thud, then silence. They then saw the other one begin wheeling himself down the flagstones. When the chair stopped, its wheels caught on the edge, he leaned forward, straining, until it finally tipped over, and he fell with it to the bottom, where the waves worked at the base of the cliff.

After that day my brain, if operating at all, was completely taken up with Musan and Michio's last trip to Izukogen, and the workings of Michio's mind during the weeks of secret planning that preceded it. I stopped going to work, and spent my days lying on the sofa, staring at a single point, hardly breathing, thinking from early morning until late at night. I sometimes spent an entire day just thinking, for instance, about the way Musan raised his hands to his ears before jumping off the edge of the cliff.

One of the sightseers on the ridge had a camera with a motor drive attached to it, and the sequence of pictures he took appeared in one of the weekly magazines. Musan's pose immediately reminded me of a photo I once saw of a sweet little boy with both hands held high in the air in a group of Jewish children being herded out of the Warsaw ghetto....

Dreams were agony, but the one blessing was that even in the worst ones, my sons didn't appear. Some power must have been protecting me from witnessing those irrevocable events which take place in the reality behind a dream. For when I went to sleep at night, what frightened me most was the idea that in the middle of a nightmare I might lose my mind, and never wake up to sanity. After a bad dream I'd wake up to find my head full of the same thoughts, though, and the pressure would drive me to my desk, where I'd sit in the dark working, not bothering with breakfast or lunch, until past noon.

Having left the textbook company, I was working for a well-known translator, preparing rough drafts for him to polish. I worked on various texts, and in the process, as my thoughts inevitably returned to that event, I came across two passages that I felt shed some light on it. The first was in a book that treated the subject of neurosis from various angles; it was a quotation from The Divine Comedy, *the opening lines of the fourth canto of the* Purgatorio.

> *When any of our senses is aroused*
> *to intensity of pleasure or of pain,*
> *the soul gives itself up to that one sense,*
> *oblivious to all its other powers.*
> *This fact serves to refute the false belief*

that in our bodies more than one soul burns.

In the notes at the back of my paperback edition of <u>The Divine Comedy</u>, I found what amounted almost to a summary of the text I was working on. "When the soul is strongly stimulated, as by joy or sadness, its powers gather into one (i.e., the capacity to feel joy or sadness); all others seem to stop functioning. Therefore, it is wrong to claim, as the Platonists do, that human beings have many souls. If that were true, even while one soul concentrated on a single object, the others would be free to turn away, and face in other directions."

That's right, I thought; if I had many souls, with one constantly grieving over the death of my sons, it would be unbearable. And when I returned to the translation, though still aware of the incident blinking on and off like a red light in the corner of my mind (but no, this is only a recent habit—even if it's one I'll have till the day I die), I was able to say to myself, right now, at this moment, my soul is concentrating on the work in front of me.

The second text I discovered in a popular history of music: a passage from the autobiography of George Sand, quoted in the chapter on her relationship with Chopin (the author gives it the usual "tragic love story" treatment). Sand and her children were living with Chopin in a monastery on the island of Majorca, some distance away from the nearest village. One day, Sand took her children down the steep mountain road into the village on some errand or other, and was caught in a bad storm. When their carriage could go no further, they left it, and got home late that night, soaked to the skin. I can't read French, so what I quote here is itself a translation:

> We were hurrying because we knew our patient would worry. His anxiety had been acute, to be sure, but by now it had frozen into calm despair, and, weeping, he was playing

54

a marvelous prelude. On seeing us come in, he rose, uttered a loud cry, then said with a wild expression and in a strange tone of voice, "Ah, just as I imagined—you died!"

... When he had recovered his senses and saw the state we were in, he realized that his mind had been unhinged by the image of us in danger. He had dreamed we were in peril, he told me later, and, no longer able to distinguish dream from reality, had calmed himself down by playing the piano. In this dream-like state, he became persuaded that he himself had died. He saw himself drowned in a lake....

I, too, am dead. Musan, also dead, pushes a wheelchair with the dead Michio in it. Leaning forward and grasping both sides of the wheelchair, I too come falling after them, onto those rocks I later saw still stained with blood. This is the scene I've been waiting for, my heart frozen in calm despair. I can see it all clearly, even my own figure, drowned, standing at the bottom of a lake....

I have copied this from various letters I received from Musan and Michio's father, editing them as I went along; and there is one more I would like to close with.

What was the driving force behind that last jump that took my two children out of this world: was it hate, or love? I've known all along that this was the heart of the problem, but whenever my thoughts seemed headed in that direction, I flinched and pulled away, as if I'd touched something boiling hot.

As I said before, Michio gradually talked Musan into it, over a certain period of time. After his accident, there was hardly anyone Michio would open up and really talk to, yet even if they did in fact have to practice using the wheelchair indoors, he spent a lot of time in Musan's room, and later on Musan started pushing him outside as well. At first both Marie and I believed that this closeness between the boys might be some compensation for Michio's pain or, going further back, for the grief Musan's birth had brought; but it was actually the groundwork for the tragedy that would come later....

There's a question that never leaves my mind. How did Michio talk Musan into suicide? He might have started by saying he wanted to go back to Izukogen, where they'd had such a good time. With Musan—just the two of them, like an adventure. As long as Musan could be counted in, they could do it.... If Michio had gone slowly, explaining everything carefully until he understood, Musan would have been eager to cooperate, proud to help this younger brother he had always looked up to.

The day the new wheelchair arrived (bought with money from my mother-in-law's inheritance), I remember Musan stroking the wheels and saying, "This is a good wheelchair—a very good wheelchair!" When he found out he'd be pushing it, he couldn't hide his delight, though he tried not to let his brother see. So if Michio had made him understand that they'd be going to Izukogen, a place he remembered as somewhere they'd had fun together, and that he, Musan, would be in charge of the wheelchair, I know he would have been thrilled.

But suicide was another matter altogether. Even so, Michio must have managed to plant the notion firmly in his brother's head, for when the wheelchair suddenly stopped—because Michio had put on the brake—it was Musan alone, in spite of all the efforts to stop him from those people on the next ridge and even Michio himself, who stuck to the original plan and threw himself off the cliff. And only then did Michio, who'd had second thoughts but was now driven by guilt at having burdened Musan with this plan of his, wheel himself forward and go through with what he'd first set out to do.

If this scene is replayed in my head, say, once every five minutes while I'm awake, that makes a couple of hundred times a day—too many thousands of times to count, all told. And what I'm left with now is the thought of how vividly Michio must have impressed on Musan the horrors of living in this world, for himself, as a paralytic, and for Musan, as a mentally handicapped child.

Musan was far more frightened of death than the average, healthy child. Whenever he had a fever or diarrhea—epileptic fits left him dazed for a while, but they were almost routine, so he was used to that—he would lie there, not daring to move, like a wounded animal. If he cut himself with a knife, he would stick his bleeding finger right under Marie's nose and then collapse, become completely helpless. And yet in this child's mind Michio instilled an anger and hatred toward the world that was strong enough to transcend his terror and make him choose to die.

"Musan, this world's a scary place! Dogs bark at you! People stare at you, and laugh! You get fits, too!" Michio's voice, whispering to Musan, sometimes echoes in my ears, as clearly as if I'm actually hearing it—probably because I did overhear him say these things (though maybe not in this order) in the dining room or the living room.

Musan particularly hated barking dogs. When one of them suddenly howled at him from behind the bushes, he was obviously terrified at first, but what I remember is the violent rage that came immediately afterward. His whole body would tense up, ready for a fight, and he'd turn to face the hidden source of that hated sound, stamp his foot, and scream, "Get him with a carving knife!"

Even while Marie and I were still separated, Michio did what he could to look after him. On the way to Shinjuku, for example, people in the train would stare at Musan as though he were a freak, which didn't seem to bother him, but Michio, furious on his behalf, used to glare back at them.

When Musan had a seizure, all we could do was lay him down on the sofa so that he wouldn't fall, and wait for it to pass. As if sharing his brother's pain, Michio used to stay at his side the whole time, looking in vain for some way to help.

These little episodes make me think that perhaps Michio, having chosen death for himself, couldn't bear to leave Musan on his own, and decided to convince him to die as well. If this is true, then Michio was burning with hatred for this world <u>and</u> love for Musan when he headed for Izukogen ... although in the end it was Michio who was left alone, if only for a few minutes, after Musan went first....

Which leads me to the realization that even for Michio, hatred and loathing couldn't have been enough to bring Musan to the point where he would actually want to die. When Musan walked on past Michio's wheelchair he had his fingers in his ears, his elbows sticking out on both sides, shutting out his brother's voice, which was telling him to stop. He wanted to go on listening to a different voice, the message Michio had repeated over and over again until it filled his head. And that, surely, would have been about the life they were going to enjoy together in the next world. Where their handicaps would suddenly vanish. For Michio, this would mean a return to life before the accident, which was straightforward enough, but how could Musan have tried to imagine himself free of his handicap? I remember once again how, whenever Musan had a fit, Michio always seemed to feel the pain along with him. Musan was aware that his physical discomfort and temporary paralysis were rooted in his mental handicap, so <u>this</u> is probably what Michio stressed, assuring him that he'd be rid of all that.

This is the scene I imagine Michio might have painted for Musan of life in the next world: Michio, his legs sound once again, and Musan, free of both his mental handicap and the physical problems that accompanied it, talking together, enjoying

58

each other's company; with Musan, of course, showing an older brother's authority, and Michio, naturally, liking it that way. (This reversion to a relationship appropriate to their ages did in fact occur, just before they jumped off that cliff in Izukogen, for the older boy jumped first, and the younger followed.)

Immediately after the incident I think Marie already had her mind made up; she would leave me, sell the house (her mother's legacy), and go off somewhere on her own. She lined our sons' pictures up on the family altar—looking at them, you could see how close the resemblance was between the retarded older brother and the bright younger one—and, without taking even a day's rest after the funeral, started clearing things out. At first it seemed she would never finish, but the day finally came when she had the boxes she was going to take with her piled up in the living room ready for the movers, and the furniture divided up as well.

It was already late at night. The heavy makeup she always wore made the fatigue stand out on her face all the more, but her eyes were almost too bright. In a low, husky voice, as she'd hardly spoken the whole time, she said to me:

"Satchan, our life was a failure—there's nothing left; the good things are all gone. From now on, whenever we see something rare or beautiful, we'll just feel all the more depressed, knowing that Musan and Michio aren't here to enjoy it with us.... I was never really that keen on Dostoevsky, but something one of his characters says came back to me a while ago, and now I can't get it out of my head. I looked it up when I found the book yesterday. It's from the scene in <u>Crime and Punishment</u> where Katerina Ivanovna takes her children out on the street corner and makes them dance and beg in the square—what she says before she finally dies. 'We have been your ruin, Sonia. Lay me down, let me die in peace. Farewell, poor thing! I am done for! I am broken!' But no matter how 'broken' I am, even if I think

59

there's nothing left for me, I can't die. If I do, you'll be the only one left to remember how Musan and Michio suffered and then died when they couldn't see any other way out. And so I'll go on living for the time being. Those lines are like a thorn in my heart, and yet they seem to give me courage somehow...."

It's almost funny to think of now, but I was so sure Marie was going to turn to me and say, "I have been your ruin, Satchan," that it made me cringe, but she just put the paperback she'd been reading from back in the cardboard box and sat there, her head tilted to one side.

"Do you really have to go? I can see why you'd want to sell this house, it's so full of their memories, but don't you think we can make a go of it somehow together?" I asked, hopefully.

"I want to be by myself, and try something I never would have done until now. And once I've done it, and about ten years have passed, I have a feeling I'll be able to 'die in peace,' quite naturally."

"Someone like you who, if she's going to raise children, raises children ... no, I really believe this, you've always put everything you had into whatever you did, and when someone like that takes on a new project, all by herself, it's bound to be special, and important. It'll be an <u>enterprise</u>. Some kind of human enterprise, in the real sense of the word."

"Enterprise, hmm...."

Marie didn't say anything more, so there was nothing for me to do but go to my room (we'd been sleeping separately) and get into bed. The next morning, when it was time for her to leave, Marie asked, as I had before, "How did Michio do it? How could he have kept at Musan for so long he actually talked him into it? My poor babies!" and then, with a wail, burst into tears; but she soon recovered, and called the real estate agent to set up an appointment. By that time it seemed that her mind was already cutting loose from the life she'd led till then.

| 4 |

As I copied down these letters from Marie's former husband, abridging them as I went along, I pictured him trapped in a dark tunnel with no way out, writing (to paraphrase a line from *Macbeth*) "so it will *not* make us mad." Novelists do, at times, receive letters like this from people they hardly know. But as Marie herself said, Satchan's weren't like anyone else's. For a while I found that, just as he describes his own situation, when I was conscious of thinking of anything at all, my mind was filled with what he'd written.

Besides, I was leading a depressing life myself at the time, alone in Mexico City. It was there that I learned, in a very strange way, of the incident involving Musan and Michio. I was under contract to teach one class a week at the Colegio de México, and my assistant, an Argentine in exile, told me about a news item concerning Japan that he'd picked up on the shortwave radio in his car. Two brothers, the older one mentally retarded, the younger in a wheelchair, had committed suicide on the Izu Peninsula. The announcer hadn't mentioned any names, my assistant said, but I gloomily reached the conclusion that these were almost certainly Marie's children.

The following week, my wife wrote and told me what had happened, and then forwarded Satchan's letters before I had a chance to send Marie my condolences. I remembered Musan outside the hunger strikers' tent with his grandmother, the time they'd come to meet his mother, an image bathed in sunlight, seen from within semidarkness.

Fear gripped me as I thought of that calm but solemn-looking boy committing suicide with his younger brother, paralyzed and in a wheelchair, and the dignified elderly lady who had preceded them in death, grieving over them to the end: fear of the brutality of passing time, of this world that scoffs, "You didn't come here by special invitation, you know—no one really needs you," and then, after wiping you out with one violent blast, goes on as if nothing had happened. The sensation I was so accustomed to in youth came flooding back to terrify me now, a middle-aged man in a foreign country.

The suicide of this retarded child immediately revived a painful memory concerning my own son. Just before I left for Mexico, my wife, usually so self-controlled, had come back from Hikari's biannual checkup almost in tears. The boy himself stood in the doorway, as subdued and docile as a domestic animal. According to my wife, while he was being examined Hikari had been "just terrible!" He had fought the nurse who was trying to take a blood sample. When the electrodes were attached to his head for a brain wave test, he had ripped them all off. The doctor had finally given up.

At the hospital, a retarded child is received warmly at first, but then sometimes, from a fear he can't suppress, he begins to resist the treatment; in my son's case, with the physical strength of a healthy boy in his late teens. The attitude of the doctors and nurses accordingly changes. The child himself is too preoccupied with his own dread to notice, but for his mother, standing by

62

watching helplessly, this is agony. To make matters worse, when the checkup had been abandoned and they were on their way home, Hikari, through no fault of his own, had one of the seizures that make life miserable for him. Then, when he got off the train with my wife's arms around him for support, his foot had slipped down into the space between the car and the platform, and it had taken all the efforts of the passengers around them to free him....

Still standing dolefully in the doorway listening to my wife, Hikari gathered his strength for one last, hopeless effort and, taking a single step forward, uttered the word "Su-i-cide...?" as though crushed by shame at the futility of his own existence. The word so shocked my wife that she immediately forgot her own exhaustion and quickly set about trying to cheer him up; and by the evening, Hikari was calmly listening to music and finding things to laugh about with his sister, so it all ended well enough....

Even a child whose mental development is defective has an understanding of suicide, and a chillingly accurate one at that; it was realizing this that made that day one of my bleakest memories. Now, hearing of Musan's death, I saw the outline of Hikari's whole person the moment he said the word "Su-i-cide," superimposed on his friend's distinctive features and mannerisms.

Before beginning the letter of condolence I would eventually have to send Marie, I tried to write a reply to her estranged husband, but didn't make much progress, and for quite some time the desk in my apartment in Mexico City was covered with half-written pages. And then it came to me. Satchan's first reason for writing to a novelist like me (as in similar cases I'd known before) was to give some shape to a collection of thoughts as tangled as brambles. But didn't he have something more specific in mind as well? Having parted again from Marie, as if blown from her side by the blast of that cruel event, Satchan would probably never find his way back to her. Nevertheless, he'd been thinking constantly about the boys' deaths, and obviously wanted to show that to her more than anyone else. Behind those letters he kept sending me, wasn't there a hidden desire to have Marie read them?

I sent Satchan's letters by airmail—coming and going, those grief-laden pages traveled across a third of the globe—back to my wife. On reading them she immediately understood, and wrote to tell me that when Marie had come over one day, she'd taken them out and encouraged her to read them. Although hesitant at first, Marie had finally relented and read each one carefully, as though determined to face what was in them head on. My wife added that although Marie still seemed exhausted, ground down by some great weight, she detected signs in her of a new, almost aggressive will to take things as they came and see them through.

"While we were still together, toward the end," Marie said, "there were moments when I was suddenly free from all those terrible thoughts; I felt so light I was almost floating. When that happened, I could see how much Satchan was suffering, but I realize now that, all along, we were both going through it the same way. From my own experience, I can't believe that going over what happened again and again, torturing ourselves like this, will help us find a way out of it. But then again, there isn't much else you can do but regret and grieve.... Anyway, it's growing into a 'poison-tree'—all this remorse."

I had a colleague at the Colegio, a ruddy-faced Englishman with melancholy blue eyes, grown stout with middle age, who had spent the past twenty years in the Americas, North and South, and was well read in his own literature. When I mentioned the "poison-tree" to him, he immediately recited the passage from Coleridge's play *Remorse* for me. I was impressed with the extent of his knowledge. But I wasn't sure what sort of sadness this man, now teaching classical economic theory to graduate students, most of whom were political exiles, had hidden deep in his ample frame along with Coleridge's gloomy verses, and since it seemed likely that once I started digging I would hit another lode of human misery, I refrained from pursuing my conversation with him in the Colegio cafeteria any further....

> Remorse is as the heart, in which it grows:
> If that be gentle, it drops balmy dews
> Of true repentance; but if proud and gloomy,
> It is a poison-tree, that pierced to the inmost
> Weeps only tears of poison!

There's a big, fat "poison-tree" growing in Marie's heart—and in Satchan's, too—I thought as I walked back to my apartment past buildings with huge clusters of bougainvillea through the dim, golden light that floated over the city. Before I knew it that "poison-tree" was spreading its branches inside me as well, and while translating Coleridge's lines into Japanese that night, I drank far too much Baja California red wine....

Marie was spending a lot of time with my wife, at home alone in Tokyo with the children. In her letters, my wife said that although she was incapable of comforting Marie in her grief, Marie was always helping her by doing little things like lending a hand with the housework. And it wasn't just that: when Hikari began having a new round of seizures, more serious than before, it was Marie who drove him to the university hospital to be examined.

So now I had to send her my thanks, along with my sympathy, and the burden of it weighed on me for several days. And then I happened to come across a letter Scott Fitzgerald wrote to a couple he'd known since they were all young together in the south of France, after they'd lost two children, one after the other. I translated the letter, not that that would have been necessary for Marie's benefit—her English was far better than mine—but as I put the words into Japanese, I felt somehow that I was writing my own letter to her.

> *Dearest Gerald and Sarah,*
>
> *The telegraph came today and the whole afternoon was so sad with thoughts of you and the past and the happy times we had once. Another link binding you to life is broken and with such insensate cruelty that it is hard to say which of the two blows was conceived with more malice. I can see the silence in which you hover now after this seven years of struggle and it would take words like Lincoln's in his letter to the mother who had lost four sons in the war to write you anything fitting at the moment. The sympathy you will get will be what you have had from each other already and for a long, long time you will be inconsolable.*
>
> *But I can see another generation growing up around Honoria and an eventual peace somewhere, an occasional port of call as we all sail deathward. Fate can't have any more arrows in its quiver for you that will wound like these. Who was it said that it was astounding how the deepest griefs can change in time to a sort of joy? The golden bowl is broken indeed but it <u>was</u> golden; nothing can ever take those boys away from you now.   Scott*

I made a clean copy for Marie from my rough draft and, adding a short postscript, a sort of footnote to the letter, sent it to her via my wife. I remember writing that I didn't believe that what Fitzgerald said about grief changing "in time to a sort of joy" would ever apply to her and Satchan. No, not even in a hundred years. Because for them it wasn't just a question of the deepest grief; it was a "poison-tree" that had taken root in them.

And I remember adding this: "Living alone here in Mexico City, I was terribly upset when a phone call came from Tokyo telling me about a seizure that had left Hikari temporarily blind, and my heart went out to him; yet even though it's an extra burden for Hikari, just knowing that he's still alive gives me the courage to go on. But you don't have that consolation, having lost both Musan and Michio at once."

Marie dropped by just when my wife was about to forward this letter, so she handed it to her. As before, after some hesitation Marie read it, and then said bluntly:

"If it wasn't for that last bit I wouldn't have had the vaguest idea what he was trying to say to me. But he's really suffering over what happened to us, isn't he? Off in Mexico by himself, poor guy ... too far away for his sympathy to really reach us here, unfortunately...."

Reading this in my wife's letter, it occurred to me that what Marie had said in Tokyo (undoubtedly not just on the spur of the moment) actually overlapped at some point with what was going through my mind in Mexico, although she and I seemed to be thinking in opposite directions. One day a week I went to the Colegio; the other six I spent in my apartment, surrounded by Spanish speakers, catching only a word or two now and then, cut off from everyone in the building. The isolation only served to deepen my anxiety when word of my son's new seizures reached me. Rationally, there was no way that brooding in the middle of the night, alone in faraway Mexico City, could possibly do anything to help him over there in Tokyo—this I knew, yet sometimes, as in a dream, I thought to myself: if only this pain inside me that never lets up could somehow, through some strange sort of sympathetic power, give him the courage to go on....

I went to a foreign bookstore in downtown Mexico City, near the intersection of the Paseo de la Reforma and the Avenida de los Insurgentes (which runs across the city—my apartment was near the north end of it) to buy as many of the novels, letters, and criticism by Marie's writer, Flannery O'Connor, as I could find. The blond, haughty woman working there, a Mexican who looked as if she had hardly a drop of New World blood in her veins, was rather cross about this, saying in heavily accented English: "Usually this writer hardly sells at all, but every once in a while someone like you, señor, comes along and buys every one of her books off the shelf. Now we'll have to reorder. There's no telling when another customer will come in looking for her works, and we have our standards to keep up!"

I then went back to the apartment and sat down to read, but I was waylaid by a passage in the introduction about lupus, the incurable disease O'Connor contracted in her youth (it wasn't until after I'd returned home that I was able to transfer the name of it into my own language). This, on top of the uncanny power of the books themselves, made the idea of Marie immersed in an emotional world like that, which offers no way out, seem almost too cruel. Without the protection of O'Connor's unyielding faith, Marie would be naked, so to speak—completely exposed to the harsh longing that filled this writer's world....

Judging from her letters, O'Connor was an intelligent woman who accepted physical suffering with cool detachment. A frank sense of humor, which perhaps came from a different temperament than her religious faith did, brightened her correspondence here and there; but I was afraid that the element of comedy, like very bright sunlight, would depress Marie all the more now. If you could compare the Izu incident to lupus, then Musan and Michio were its victims. And while it was necessary to get up the courage it took to face the effects of lupus, what good could that possibly do Marie now?

In the end I decided to leave O'Connor for later, and turned instead to Andrei Bely's *The Silver Dove* (part of a series of early twentieth-century Russian authors), which I'd bought along with the other books, and was soon swept up in it: Russia on the eve of the revolution, when the burgeoning energy of the masses, as yet without any clear direction, was shaking firmly embedded Orthodox beliefs to their roots; the passions and dreams of a young man from the city who wanders into a Russian village in just such a crisis; and the pockmarked servant, Matryona, who seduces him, drawing him into her religious sect. The spell she cast on me was so strong I could feel it right in the pit of my stomach.

When I fell asleep after reading until dawn, the dream I had, obviously influenced by Bely, was so sensual I thought twice about recording it in the simple diary I'd been keeping in Mexico. I was past forty then, but this was the first time I'd been away from home for longer than three months since I'd been married. In the dream, Marie appeared as previously described, with her hair wet after swimming at the sports club. Her face, too sharply defined to be a young woman's, was covered (as though this were perfectly natural) with pockmarks. I somehow knew that these were scars left by the loss of Musan and Michio. They gave her a coarse sensuality I hadn't seen before; but her eyes shone with the pure light of an inner resolution. Bely had written, I remembered, that Matryona's pockmarked face, sensual to the point of vulgarity, "radiated a pure, sapphire light, like the keening sound of bagpipes," when she whispered words of love to the young man.

In the dream, the sound of Marie's name was strangely close to Matryona. With only a tulle shawl over her shoulders, and her round Betty Boop breasts bare, she sat, naked from the waist down, on a black plastic pipe chair with her legs tightly crossed. I was standing in front of her, but on a lower level, so that my head was level with her knees. Marie gazed down at me, as though at a child. She had something to say, and I was meant to listen quietly. No interruptions from me would be tolerated; the mocking smile that played about her lips dismissed them as puerile before I had a chance to open my mouth.

Marie's left thigh, resting on the other, was drawn up so high the lower part of her genitals should have showed, but the whole area was hidden by a sort of devil's tail, seen upside down—actually thick black pubic hair that curled around it, covering it completely. It was partly Matryona, the temptress, who conjured up this image in my dream; but I also remembered something from that time when Marie passed me in the pool, her thighs scissoring through the water: a glimpse of dark pubic hair, floating free, or plastered to the inside of her groin....

"God (or maybe you'd prefer 'the cosmic will') took my poor children away from me," Marie said in the dream, moving those bright red Betty Boop lips of hers. "And he did it in a horrible way. He made it look as if they'd decided to die on their own, but they were so young, how could they have just slipped over to the other side like that without being tempted? God planned it all, and now I'm going to get my revenge. If he's supposed to be promoting 'good,' then I'll do the opposite—do 'bad,' deliberately. Which is why I'm dressed this way, to look the part, at least to begin with. But I just can't seem to get things moving.

"I never once thought of Musan's handicap as something 'evil' inflicted on me. I always considered it an accident. Musan used to lie on the carpet in the living room listening to Mozart, and I'd be sitting there on the sofa, watching him; and at times like that I'd say to myself, we're on our way to recovering from the accident. And then when Michio had *his* accident and came home in a wheelchair, he was unbelievably kind to me; even when despair got the better of him and he was irritable or angry, if the two of us could be alone, he'd be all right.... I think Michio and I were beginning to recover from that accident, too.

"But then they were stolen away, both of them. There's no recovering from something like that. It's the real thing—'evil'—and I'm the one it was done to. It may look as if it was done just to Musan and Michio, but I'm the one who has to go on living, feeling the pain. And so I'm going to start something of my own, an enterprise, something big enough to avenge this 'evil.' The trouble is, the world we live in" (Marie in the dream actually looked as though she'd already crossed the threshold between this world and the next; a witch played by Betty Boop) "doesn't offer much opportunity for doing something really 'evil.' Say I seduced a couple of men and then jilted them, made them die of a broken heart (hard to imagine these days). I'd make their families suffer too, of course, but that's as far as it would go, isn't it?

"On the official scale of 'evil,' the worst thing we can do is a crime we'd be arrested and executed for eventually. But how would it rate on *my* scale? Say I do a certain amount of 'evil'—we'll call it x—which earns me the death sentence—we'll call it x'; when x and x' are about equal, then I suppose the public, at least, is satisfied with the outcome. All right. Now, what if I'd done something out of all proportion to the weight of the death sentence—if it was $x > x'$? The judge and executioner might be too disgusted even to want to kill me; but they couldn't very well go on sentencing me to death, over and over again, until the unequal equation was reversed, $x < x' + x'' + x'''$ ... could they? You see, the point I'm trying to make is that no amount of 'evil' on my part could ever equal the figure represented by my poor babies being snatched away from me....

"So tell me—what can I possibly do, from where I am now, to get back at god? Just trying to imagine an 'evil' that great is like chasing clouds.... But I can't give up now. I'll start with some dry runs—give them everything I've got—there's nothing else I can come up with for the moment. And you, K, how long are you planning to stay here, hiding in Mexico? Hurry up and come back. If you'd like, I can tickle you with my pitchfork, you might enjoy that."

When she had finished talking, Marie slid around on the seat of her chair until she was facing backward, gripping the backrest between her knees, the black tail of pubic hair setting off her flawless skin, white even to the crotch; and, slowly rising, she floated away, disappearing amid the glittering lights of the night sky above the city....

With a deep sadness and a massive hard-on, the kind I used to get when I was eighteen or nineteen, and not knowing what to do with either, I opened my eyes to the dismal Mexican morning beyond the cheap curtains of my room. But then I thought I heard a scream from the sky into which the witch had vanished, the shriek Marie had let out when faced with the bodies of Musan and Michio at the police station in Ito (described in a letter from Satchan), which had echoed throughout the building; and the seductive image of Betty Boop faded from my mind....

5

Marie came over one Sunday late the year I returned from Mexico. When I overheard my wife explaining to her on the phone that I had arrived the day before yesterday but was still tired and suffering from jet lag, I asked her to have Marie come anyway, as originally planned. Recently she'd been at our house every Sunday, giving Hikari some coaching in piano and composition. For three years now he'd been studying music with the wife of an editor, an old friend of mine, but his teacher had gone to Vienna the previous summer for a short training course, and, following the basic pattern of her lessons, Marie was filling in for her.

After the Izu incident, Marie had quit her job at the women's university. Hoping that regular work of some kind would keep her mind occupied, my wife had first asked her to teach our daughter and younger son English conversation, but they were unwilling recruits, and didn't put much effort into it. Having dragged Marie into this, knowing—partly, in fact, because she knew—that she was in a very bad way, physically as well as emotionally, my wife didn't know what to do at that point. But all this time a sense of rivalry had been building in Hikari as he watched his younger siblings monopolize their beautiful teacher, and on English conversation days she noticed how diligent he was about working on his music. Marie was immediately interested, especially in helping him with harmony and melody.

Marie had gone to a private junior high school well known for its music program, and had planned to major in music after high school. But when her grandfather started up a business in America and put her father in charge of operations there, she had transferred to a high school in New York, and the language problem had forced her to abandon the piano. The day she learned Hikari was likely to be deprived of his music lessons for a while, Marie dropped in to see his piano teacher, who was busy getting ready for her trip, and made arrangements to continue them in her absence. Thus we were able to have Hikari go on with the lessons that were the main joy in his life, while at the same time freeing his younger brother and sister from English conversation.

With Marie talking patiently to him the whole time, Hikari would write out a melody and set harmony to it in long, drooping notes that looked like bean sprouts. Since Hikari's fingers, affected by his handicap, are too clumsy for him to play the piano with any skill, she would then play the new piece for him, instructing and encouraging him as she did so. They were hard at work when I woke up late and came downstairs from my study that day. Without speaking to Marie, I went straight to my luggage from Mexico (I'd started unpacking a couple of days before) with the hopeless feeling that no greeting would have been appropriate after what had happened.

My Mexican students had given me a Huichol Indian yarn painting, mounted on a plywood base, which I'd folded in two when I packed it. While I was reattaching the strands of yarn that had come loose at the fold, the lesson ended, and Marie, dispensing, as I had, with any preliminary greetings as she stepped down from the dining room where the piano was, said:

"Those colors are lovely—psychedelic, as they used to say. Seems everything that strikes us as new and original they've already got in Mexico or South America, and they've had it since ancient times, long before we even thought of the word 'psychedelic'...."

"I heard that if you look at it after taking a mild hallucinogen, like the hippies used to do, these greens and yellows and reds really do make you see things...."

"Don't the Huichol Indians go up into the hills to dig up a kind of cactus that has that effect? As an initiation journey. I saw something about it on television. You know, you've lost a lot of weight, K. Your initiation journey took a lot out of you, didn't it?"

"Hikari said, 'Papa has become very thin!'" my wife added, and my son, who always knows when he's being talked about, stopped in the middle of putting away his practice music to smile at me.

But then I took a good look at Marie for the first time, and realized that it was she who had become very thin, as though that pockmarked mask in my dream in Mexico had suddenly been removed, leaving the eyes as they were, shining with a pure light, but revealing a face that was darkened by the sun and painfully drawn. Without mentioning the incident, Marie started asking questions about my life in Mexico. She had wanted to go there herself ever since she'd studied Spanish at high school in New York. The only information Marie had to offer about herself was that she had joined a small study group at a Catholic church. There were in fact two groups, one for older people and the other for the young; although she was somewhere in between, she'd joined the younger one for the time being. Compared to the other women there, whose aim was to move toward belief—studying, in other words, in order to confirm the fact of god's existence—

75

she felt she was … well, actually, the same up to a point, but, looking beyond, far off into the distance, quite different.…

"I've been reading Flannery O'Connor for a long time now without ever really considering whether god exists or not. After all, her novels do permit that sort of reading. But now I want an actual experience of the 'mystery' she talks about; to know what it feels like. Just to touch the edge, so that I can say to myself, oh, so that's what it is, and then come right back. I'll only stay on the other side long enough to brush past it. I'm curious—I feel like a spy. Too bad for the priest, though, giving all this guidance to a nonbeliever, a trespasser, in a way."

"He's probably used to people like that, you know. They say that when the first churches were built early in the Meiji era, while Christianity was still prohibited, a certain percentage of the believers were actually Buddhist spies from the Nichiren sect. That was over a hundred years ago, but still …"

"But don't some people start out that way, and then after listening to the priest for a while, actually begin to believe?" my wife said.

"If that happened to me, I'm afraid it would just complicate things even more. I'll have to be careful not to let myself go."

I could tell by the expression on Marie's face, as she stood there looking at the yarn painting, that she had no wish to continue this conversation; she seemed lost on some dark, winding pathway inside herself. When she turned and walked toward the door, there was nothing my wife and I could do but watch her go in silence. Only Hikari saw her off with a gentle "Good-bye," trying to lighten the mood that had suddenly closed in on us.…

I had a vague understanding of what Marie meant by the word "mystery" from O'Connor's critical essays which I'd reread, or seen for the first time, after that bizarre dream in Mexico. But my copy of *Mystery and Manners*, along with most of the books I'd bought in Mexico, was on its way across the Pacific at the time, making it impossible to go up to my study and check it right away.... Even so, her concept of the novel, as a concrete description of manners through which moments of a transcendent vision are revealed, was one I felt I had grasped clearly enough.

O'Connor maintains that only when we conceive of the natural world as good can we clearly understand evil, and the thought of this young woman writer, forsaken by the "good" in this world, struggling against a fatal illness, filled me with respect for her. Wasn't it because Marie had lost the greatest "good" in her life, her children, that she was now having trouble seeing where "evil" was ... despite her desperate efforts to perceive "mystery" in the image of Musan plunging off the cliff in the pose of a child being led from the Warsaw ghetto to the gas chamber, with Michio following after, furiously wheeling himself over the edge?... But these were just random thoughts running through my head without any logical connection, and with very little knowledge or experience of religion, I was still pretty much in the dark. I had merely begun to pick up a few vague hints from Marie's writer.

With the work of a different writer as a medium, I had a chance to talk to Marie about what had happened to her children the following week, after Hikari's lesson. That morning, a man in his thirties who claimed to be a freelance journalist had descended on her apartment, apparently, and given her an awful time. As she told us about it, still seething with rage, the conversation led naturally back to Izu. Without telling her what magazine he was from, he had informed her he was going to do an article on the incident—which Marie referred to as "it"—and asked for an interview. This resulted in their having what was from Marie's point of view an incredibly depressing and unproductive argument through the gap in the front door (fortunately the chain was on).

She had told him she was still suffering from the pain and

shock of it—there was no point in saying she didn't want to remember it, since it was something she would never forget—and had no desire to talk about it with someone she'd never seen before, and then have to read her own words again in some magazine or other. What good could yet another news story on the subject possibly do her, she'd protested. Ignoring her question, the writer had only made her angrier still by saying that the pictures in the weeklies just after the incident had been thoroughly depressing, and asking for photographs of her with the children "in happier days."

When she refused to offer either pictures or comments (he'd been taping her the whole time without telling her), he had warned her that an article written only on the basis of the conversation so far would leave his readers with the impression of "an emotionally unstable mother with a domineering personality." He could get the shots he needed easily enough by making the rounds of the boys' classmates, so it really didn't make any difference whether they came from her or not, but since they were going to appear in the magazine anyway, wouldn't she rather they were ones she liked?...

When Marie had asked why articles like this were necessary in the first place, he had replied, claiming to be an expert on educational problems, that it was to expose the hell our children are going through as the education system breaks down. And, sure enough, when she'd checked the mail on her way out that afternoon, there had been a book he'd written on educational problems in her mailbox....

"Isn't there anything you can do to keep a story like that—obtained through invasion of someone's privacy—from coming out?" my wife asked.

"I'm afraid not, even if you could find out where it was going to be published," I said, feeling singularly useless.

Marie sighed in obvious disappointment. "Instead of all these horrible articles they keep foisting on me, I'd much rather read a good novel with a character who's experienced something of the same kind in it. I've been trying to think of one for a while now, but with no luck. Any suggestions?"

"Well, I can't tell you anything about English literature, obviously, but in French, Balzac's *Le Curé de village* might be just what you're looking for. In fact, I had it in mind while I was in Mexico."

"You spent a lot of time thinking about that in Mexico, didn't you?… If you've got it in translation I'd like to borrow it."

After I'd found the volume in Balzac's Complete Works and handed it over, I told Marie and my wife the story. I had come across a copy of the Collection Folio paperback in Mexico City, and reread it for the first time since I was a student twenty years before, so it was still fresh in my memory.

The setting is Limoges, at the beginning of the nineteenth century. A man who has made a fortune dealing in scrap iron marries a woman whose peasant vitality shows in her *grosse encolure* (thick neck). The daughter born to them is blond and very beautiful, known throughout the neighborhood as "la petite Vierge." But at the age of eleven the girl comes down with smallpox and loses her beauty. (When I reached this part of the story, I realized that Marie's face in my dream, that rubber mask poked full of holes, had been suggested not only by the pockmarked skin of Matryona, the village witch, but also by Véronique, scarred for life by this childhood illness.) Even with her face ravaged by smallpox, however, the girl retains her elegance and grace, and Balzac tells us that she is seized with such fervor when taking Holy Communion, her pitted skin recovers its purity.

Her father arranges for her to marry a banker, already an old man. Véronique's life now centers around the intellectual pleasures of her salon, where the best people in Limoges gather, and her charity work. The years pass, and she astonishes her friends by becoming pregnant with her elderly husband's child. Around the same time, in the same region, a factory worker named Tascheron is tried and sentenced to death for killing the owner of an orchard he was trying to rob. The news is a terrible shock to Véronique.

After her husband's death, Véronique leaves Limoges for the village of Montegnac, in the surrounding hills. With the cooperation of the curé, M. Bonnet, who has been practicing his own brand of Catholicism in the village, and a failed architect unable to adjust to a bureaucratic society, she undertakes a vast public works enterprise, irrigating the sandy, rocky soil, turning it into rich farmland. During the long years of work on this project, she subjects herself to various privations, wearing horsehair next to her skin, and eating almost nothing. Her health ruined, on the verge of death, Véronique begs the curé to allow her to hold a "public confession," at which she reveals her role in Tascheron's crime and the fact that her son was conceived in adultery with him. With the knowledge that she will now finally be able to atone for her sin, Véronique's radiant beauty is restored....

"So in Véronique's case the sin came first, and she devoted her whole life to atoning for it.... But surely what happened to Marie has got nothing to do with committing a sin—can't you see that?" my wife protested, a desire to defend her friend reinforcing her own natural reaction. Marie took up the challenge where she left off.

"No, I think he meant to draw a parallel between the two catastrophes, my loss and Véronique's smallpox. So you've got it all figured out, have you, K? You think I'm going to commit a mortal sin sometime soon, adultery perhaps, with a murder lurking in the background, is that it?"

I sat there in silence, unable to defend myself against these two formidable women.

"I'll still borrow *Le Curé de village*, though. I'm sure Balzac puts plenty of passion into his description of Véronique's land project, and that's what I really want to read. If I have any hope at all of escaping from the effect of all this, getting involved in some public works project may be the only way. Assuming, of course, that it'd be possible for someone like me to get involved in a big enterprise like that nowadays...."

Marie put the huge book in her bag with the sheet music and went home. After she'd left I thought things over, and realized how presumptuous it had been on my part to draw a connection between *Le Curé de village* and the tragedy in Marie's life as I sat there reading in my room in Mexico City—even if it had seemed all the more vivid in the atmosphere of that lonely apartment, with no furniture but a black wooden chair and a bed, and nothing for decoration except the long, slender wooden mask of a boy's face that I'd bought at the market in Tosca, and the books that lined the walls....

Then one day Asao and his friends came to see me on their own, and what they had to say made me painfully aware of the gap between my half-baked assumptions and the suffering Marie had been through since the Izu incident.

The three had graduated from university in March. Having spent their college years together, it would have been a letdown to split up after graduation, so they stuck together and formed a team, on the lookout for something different as a way of life (like so many of their generation). Asao came from a *zainichi* Korean family—I hadn't known this before, but his given name was written with the character for "Korea"—and considering the prejudice he was liable to encounter when he looked for a job, they had all decided not to try a career in business. Their preference was for film production, and they were now preparing themselves for it guerrilla-style, taking on any jobs that would give them the experience they needed and refusing everything else.

Though the distinctive creases and hollows determined by

family lineage would no doubt appear as they grew older, all three still had the egg-smooth faces of youth, unmarked by any hardship; yet they were utterly serious about the matter they wanted to discuss with me. It seemed Marie's present psychological state was worrying them.

To sum up what they said—not that any of them talked very much: although Marie had acted like her lively old self when I saw her (except for the darkness in her expression), it had apparently taken a tremendous effort. At home in her apartment near Sengawa Station on the Keio Line, she was living like somebody suffering from severe clinical depression. With the curtains drawn to shut out the light, she would lie all day on the sofa staring into space, with eyes that glowed as if the irises were ringed with phosphorescence. Even the trip downstairs to fetch the mail seemed too much for her; and on clear days she made a point of keeping her head turned away from the green leaves, bathed in sunlight outside—when she had loved plants more than anything before....

"At night you can hear her pacing in her room upstairs," Asao said, the sadness in his eyes, fixed on a point in space, contrasting with his ruddy cheeks and trendy moustache.

There was a reason why they had such detailed information about Marie's daily life, even at night. She had sold the house where she'd lived with the family and, using the money left over after paying inheritance tax on the property, which had been her mother's, she had bought a condominium in Sengawa. It was a two-story building divided into three apartments. Marie had bought two, offering one rent-free to Asao and his friends as a base for their work, provided they paid the maintenance fee plus utilities. Although all three were there only in the daytime, somebody almost always stayed on at night and, through the door that joined the two apartments on the first floor, knew roughly what was going on next door....

"The shock to Marie—from the outside, I mean—is impossible to imagine and, to begin with, I don't think any of us really understood it." This was apparently something they had already discussed among themselves. Asao went on, thinking as he talked: "We've used her experience as the plot for a scenario, as a way of coming to grips with it on our own terms. We managed to take the story from the time when she was living with Musan, to when Michio had his accident, then on to what happened at Izukogen, and that's where we hit a dead end.

"The problem is that we don't know what kind of damage she's suffered inside. And it's even harder to imagine how she can possibly put her life back together after such a shattering experience. Maybe not her life so much as something more basic—how she can reconstruct herself.... So our plot is like an old movie when the reel breaks; it suddenly stops, and then nothing.... But we want to do whatever we can to help her out of this depression....

"We haven't told Marie, but we contacted somebody at the company her grandfather set up about some little things that've come up since she's been alone, and, through him, we found out what's been going on with her kids' father, that guy she calls Satchan. He's a total wreck. He's become an alcoholic, and doesn't seem to have the will to get back on his feet. It would really hurt Marie if she knew. Because when Satchan said he wanted to bring Michio and move back in, she told him OK for convenience's sake, knowing all the time she didn't love him any more, and that's been weighing on her....

"Even if we can't keep Satchan from destroying himself, we don't want Marie to go the same route.... So what should we do?"

I had no answer to give them.

"The plot of that scenario you were just telling me about, which you wrote as a way of thinking about Marie's life. It broke off in the middle, and then nothing? Just a blank screen?"

"In the last scene we want to show her a little older, living in peace, but we don't know how to get there," Asao said glumly, no longer hoping for any clear advice from me.

My wife, who had been listening quietly, broke the silence.

"Remember that Balzac novel you lent Marie? She told me she'd seen a connection with what happened to Musan and Michio while she was reading it. Don't you think you should tell them about it? Marie might take a hint from the story, and start in on something new.... And when that happens, they'd better be ready for it, don't you think?"

I could hear the lingering resentment that lay behind my wife's words; her angry protest when I first recommended *Le Curé de village* to Marie, that her friend's tragedy had no relation to what Véronique's sin had brought about. I wanted to explain to Asao and his friends how, alone in that gloomy apartment in Mexico City, I had linked Marie and Véronique in my mind without any logical justification for it—though the terror I'd felt, thinking that if my own child were to commit suicide, the blow would be far more devastating than any sin I'd ever been guilty of, might be considered a psychological justification.

"Véronique, the heroine of the novel, has the trauma of getting smallpox as a child, and being disfigured by it. By the ending, however, when she's on her deathbed and gets permission to make a 'public confession,' she's described as looking pure and full of life, as though she'd returned to the time when she was called 'la belle madame Graslin.' That was how people referred to her when she was a married woman, devoted to charity work, with her own salon. The name, and descriptions of how her face would suddenly regain its radiance in moments of religious ecstasy when she was a girl, foreshadow her final transfiguration in the 'public confession' scene.

"So the beauty of a face that's been destroyed is recovered at the end of life; the impossible becomes possible. Dickens's *Bleak House*, written around the same time, has a similar motif, so having a face ruined by smallpox must have been a fairly common tragedy for young girls back then.

"But aside from the problem of smallpox, there's Véronique's own awareness of having sinned. She commits adultery, which leads to a murder. Her lover, Tascheron, plans a robbery to get money so they can escape to the New World together, and winds up killing the man he's trying to steal it from. Véronique herself is there at the scene of the crime, but by keeping it secret, she ruins her lover's chances of having extenuating circumstances taken into account. That sense of sin drives her to wear sackcloth under her clothes, restrict herself to a starvation diet, and put all her energy into a plan to improve a stretch of arid land.

"And all that's superimposed on Balzac's motif of beauty being restored to a face that's been ruined. Without this sense of sin, Véronique couldn't have regained the radiance that smallpox had spoiled; in other words, she couldn't have managed to make the impossible happen. . . .

"Now, in Marie's case, first she has a handicapped child, then his younger brother is crippled in an accident, and finally the two of them commit suicide together. When I was in Mexico and heard what had happened, it occurred to me that having such an unbelievable series of disasters come crashing down on you might be something like being suddenly disfigured by smallpox—only a lot worse, of course. . . .

"For Marie, recovering from her pain will be a huge undertaking, like making the impossible possible. That's what you were trying to do in your scenario, wasn't it?—to imagine the process of healing the soul. And then you suddenly found yourselves up against a brick wall.

"Balzac might give you a hint about how to carry the story further along; his way of using Véronique's sense of sin as a sort of

85

lever to begin the healing process, I mean. After having her children die like that—which, as my wife says, of course, isn't something Marie should feel responsible for—but then again, along with all the remorse, she's bound to have *some* sense of sin, isn't she? That's what the three of you were worried about in the first place.... It's incredibly sad, though. Anyway, I had this vision of Marie using her sense of sin as a lever, and starting out on some new enterprise; and in the process, I thought maybe the impossible would become possible...."

"Enterprise—we heard Marie use that word, too, didn't we?" Asao said, turning to his friends for confirmation. "Does the novel give a detailed description of that farmland project?"

I got out the edition with the relief map of Montegnac to show them. Then I explained the scene, a barren wasteland at the foot of a great forest with a river flowing through it—described with the same passion Balzac devotes to major characters like Véronique —and the plan, conceived by an architect who reminded me of the leaders of the student movement during the sixties, and how it was carried out; seeing, for no logical reason, a certain affinity in temperament between this young architect and Asao and his friends....

"This is quite a project," said the one who was most interested in the map. "But if there was a river that flooded its banks every year when the rains came, and bedrock that could be used to channel off the excess water, I'm sure they could've pulled it off. Even without machines, the farmers would've been a dedicated work force, and they had financial backing too."

"Ko'ichi was in a seminar on river embankment at university," explained Asao. "But by the time we graduated, there were enough dams to produce electricity, and even the big ones that used to keep over a hundred people employed are now being operated by two or three guys who know something about computers...."

"Things might be different abroad, but here in Japan I don't think anybody's into topographical reform for farmland any more," said Ko'ichi. "If Marie wants to start a project like this, working with farmers, I'm afraid she'll have a hard time finding one."

"Yeah, but it doesn't have to be public works. If we get her to the point where she's got the energy to start something—anything—we'll be on the right track.... No matter how it turns out, it'll be better than having her moaning and pacing the floor like a sleepwalker all night." This came from Toru, the quietest of the three, who spoke up for the first time that day; in fact, I had never heard his voice before. Evidently a passionate introvert, he was now so wrought up that his eyes were red around the rims.

They all warmly thanked my wife for having mentioned *Le Curé de village*, and then left.

When Hikari had his next lesson, Marie didn't tell me what she thought of the book; she didn't have a chance, as I was busy with a guest when they finished, and we simply said hello in passing. Soon after that, Hikari's music teacher returned to Japan, putting an end to Marie's weekly visits.

After playing the short piece Hikari had written under Marie's instruction, his teacher said that, compared to his previous compositions, it had a deep sadness in it, and when she played it over for us, my wife and I agreed. The music had obviously grown out of Marie's grief, projected in turn onto Hikari. Technically, though, all Marie had done was correct it whenever it departed from the basic rules of composition; both the melody and harmony were Hikari's own creation....

At our suggestion, he gave each new piece a title, to make it easier to keep his music in order, and after writing out a clean copy, he filed it away under that title. Until now there had been lots of "Waltzes" and "Sicilianos," but, whether he had discussed it with Marie or thought of it himself, the score my wife found in the paper holder was called "Memories of Musan."

| 6 |

The three who came to me for advice that day, moved solely by goodwill and a desire to help Marie get over her depression, were definitely men of the new age: as a member of the older generation, all I could do was talk about her problem in the abstract, but within six months they had already started on their own project, centered around Marie.

Their plan was to invite a Filipino theater group to Japan for performances, including lectures by the director/male lead, not only in Tokyo but all over the country. They would avoid large public halls, moving the young Filipino's plays around a "grass-roots" network of college classrooms and meeting rooms in libraries with a capacity of one or two hundred at the most....

I went to one of these performances, held at a university campus that had been moved from central Tokyo out to a hill overlooking Mitaka. Before the play began, Marie and the group's leader walked out among the simple props on the stage, each carrying a chair. Small and wiry but extremely expressive, the leader spoke calmly in English with a Filipino accent, which Marie smoothly interpreted into Japanese. He was performing under a stage name, a Tagalog word meaning "cosmic will" which I'm afraid I didn't catch. But at the party afterward everyone was calling him Coz, so that's how I'll refer to him.

A man of about thirty, Coz was the same size as Marie, sitting beside him. His movements were quick and graceful, as though he'd trained at some sport that kept you limber without making you muscle-bound. It seemed he was raising money for his group by taking their works-in-progress abroad and lecturing on the side. Immediately drawn in by his sense of humor and skill as a storyteller, I was sure he'd do very well. He was dressed in jeans and a denim jacket with silk embroidery across the front and around the sleeves. The poppy-colored shirt and jade pendant, enclosed in a square silver frame, added to the effect, setting off his handsome face and the beard sprouting from his chin—the kind Confucian scholars in Korea used to have.

Coz told us about how he had been born in a farming village, hours by bus from any large city like Manila. He had grown up listening avidly to VOA radio broadcasts, collecting scrap metal for the local blacksmith from anti-aircraft emplacements the Japanese had left, bravely gritting his teeth when he was circumcised by the amateur doctor in the village....

The play, which began after Marie had withdrawn, leaving Coz alone on the stage, was based on these childhood memories ... the atmosphere of Christianity, now firmly rooted in Filipino soil ... bananas amid the tropical/semitropical foliage painted on the backdrop, so vivid one caught a sweet, sultry smell coming from it ... Coz and the others, slipping freely back and forth between the past and the present, and then the appearance of Uncle Sam, a youthful Peace Corps worker who offered to send Coz to the States. The American boy who played this part looked like a young Lincoln, wearing a top hat decorated with the stars and stripes. And, abruptly, these sketches of village life turned into a grotesque allegory of Coz in America, having his first collision with foreign culture....

After escaping from that bizarre experience, Coz had begun performing his autobiographical play as student drama in the university section of Manila. But then it was "discovered" by an American film director making a movie about the Vietnam War on location in the Philippines, and the play was exported, along with Coz himself, back to America. That was the "cosmic will" at work. It had also been the "cosmic will" that made American customs officials take the scenery and props he'd sent by sea mail for a pile of junk from an old shed somewhere and throw the lot away. "Because that was what changed our whole style of performance," Coz said by way of a conclusion, drawing the curtain across the stage....

Afterward, Asao and his friends helped some of the students from the university load the lighting equipment, the horizontal bar from which the backdrop had hung, and the few pieces of scenery into the rear of the jeep I remembered from before. While they were working, Marie introduced me to Coz, and we talked on the way to her apartment in Sengawa, but within thirty minutes we were there. Impressed at the efficiency of the system that had brought the Cosmic Will group to the Japanese stage, I asked Coz if things went this smoothly when they performed at American universities or at home in Manila. "No," he said, "the Japanese do everything so quickly; and here the 'cosmic will' works with a competence that's very Japanese." The expression in his eyes, deep and mysterious as pools of amber, might have been either admiration or bewilderment....

We had a party in the living room on the first floor, drinking beer straight out of cans like American students, with an avocado dip Marie whipped up to go with the potato chips. Having turned the other apartment over to the Cosmic Will, Asao and his friends were now using this area as an office and meeting room. We ate and drank sitting on the floor, surrounded by the piano, a television, and stacks of video tapes.

In the next room, a shelf had been installed by the dining room table; on it was a weird yet whimsical-looking paper angler fish, about a meter long, done in Japanese ink, and a set of six-sided tea cups. Fastened with tacks to the wall next to it was a long, narrow length of cloth, made of skeins of indigo and white thread tied together with string. I remembered hearing that Michio had made the things on the shelf, while the cloth was Musan's work....

Although Asao and his friends were handling the business side of Coz's Japan tour—it had taken them a while to park the jeep and put away the equipment, so they arrived late and were now sitting quietly by the wall—it was Marie who had heard about him from an American friend, and suggested inviting his group to visit Japan on their way home.

"It must've been the 'cosmic will' working on Marie, drawing her attention to us; there's no other way to explain it. Manila–San Francisco–Tokyo. Suddenly there was a route that connected all three, just like that," Coz said, giving me his version of how they had come to be here.

Marie nodded as she listened, directing a dark look of great intensity at me that said, if all this grief I've been carrying around with me since before that thing was just a scheme the 'cosmic will' cooked up to get me to invite some Filipinos to Japan, I'll go out of my mind. But then, as though to escape these painful thoughts for a moment, she spoke aloud. Her English was as fluent as Uncle Sam's, the young American whom everyone was addressing by his name in the play:

"Coz, I hope the 'cosmic will' keeps on working for you, so the powers that be don't find out you're all working on tourist visas. Asao tried to get you the right kind of visa but couldn't, since you came straight from America. It would be awful if you were charged with working here illegally and never allowed to come back. Just when the Japan Foundation's considering giving you a grant...."

The telephone on the dining room table rang. Marie took her time about answering it, and then strolled back into the living room and spoke to Asao. In contrast to her casual manner, he and his friends jumped up and rushed outside. She then told me what it was about. The apartment complex was situated on the grounds of a temple, with some ancient trees left standing, which made for a pleasant setting. There were three buildings in a row, each one built slightly behind the next. The priest, who was also the caretaker, lived in one of them with his family, and the others had each been divided into three two-story condos. Marie had bought two of the condos in the middle building; the third was owned by the priest, who had rented it out to a Canadian businessman. Even since the theater group had moved in, there had been a steady stream of complaints from the Canadian. Playing records or the piano after ten o'clock was now out of the question; even parties had to end before then. That had been him on the phone just now, complaining that the jeep with the stage scenery in it was taking up too much space in the parking lot.

"If he's being unreasonable, why not have a word with the priest and tell him your side of the story?"

"Oh, I'm sure he's right about the jeep being over the line. Besides, my car's there, too. All they're going to do is park it on the street to get it out of the way for a while. They'll put it back later. There've been rehearsals and parties here till two or three every morning lately, so it's only natural that he should feel a bit persecuted. The old priest doesn't really know what to make of it all." There was a hint of wry embarrassment in Marie's eyes, which, now that she'd lost so much weight, had a slightly foreign look to them, with folds in the lids. "There's something else that's been annoying the Canadian and the people in the place next door," she added, "and it has everything to do with me."

At this point, Asao and his companions returned, their earlier haste now replaced by an equivalent composure. They'd not only moved the jeep to a more suitable parking space, but had also remembered to bring the paper bag of groceries they'd left in the driver's seat. For dinner, the visiting actors and actresses were going to cook some Filipino dishes.

Marie then asked me up to her living quarters on the second floor. Her study was at the top of the stairs. Hanging on the wall was a photograph of Flannery O'Connor on crutches, looking down on a flock of peacocks gathered around the porch of her wood frame house. O'Connor's own works and books about her were lined up in the bookcase next to it, along with a collection of English paperbacks, some of them probably left over from Marie's high school days in America.

Among the few Japanese books was a novel of mine about my family, in which I'd tried to draw a connection between the metaphors in Blake's poetry and Illuminated Plates and the inner life of my handicapped son. There was also a reproduction (a good one, it seemed to me) of Orc, the figure personifying youth in Blake's mythical world, with arms outspread, on top of Marie's well-organized desk.

"I didn't bring you up here to show you the study of a phony scholar who hardly does any research. Go into the bedroom. Don't turn on the light, just walk straight through and look out the window, down and to your left. You should be able to see someone under the plane tree by the building in front of this one, at the corner of the main road."

The darkness in the room had the soft, fragrant air of a place inhabited by a mature woman alone. I reached the window, with its curtains drawn, and looked down to see a tall, thin man standing near the building, swaying slowly from side to side, staring up at me. He had a paper bag in one hand which he seemed to rub against his mouth from time to time, apparently sipping from a bottle inside. For someone as drunk as he was, he was behaving with a certain moderation.

I returned to the study, walking more confidently now that my eyes were used to the dark, to find Marie standing by the desk with her head down, restlessly fiddling with the frame of the Blake reproduction.

"Could you tell it was Satchan?" she said in a subdued voice.

"Musan and Michio's father?... I can see why he'd be a nuisance to the people living in that building, but then he's really not the type of drunk you'd want to call the police about...."

"He's being fairly quiet tonight. One time he had a tape of Beethoven's Ninth and was singing along with it. When he's sober, Satchan's just an average guy, not much trouble to anyone, so if the police do come and take him away, they soon let him go. And the next day he's back again."

Unable to think of anything else to say, we went back downstairs. Uncle Sam, sitting on the floor drinking a can of beer, his long legs poking up on either side of him like a grasshopper, stared straight at me, a penetrating look in his blue eyes.

The young men and women from the Philippines had formed their own group and were happily making preparations for dinner. They had laid the food out on a vinyl sheet on the floor by the dining room table, and were sitting in a circle around it, singing in harmony as they worked, laughing aloud from time to time. Meanwhile, Asao and his friends were going over the schedule for the Kyushu tour, to begin the following week, occasionally going next door to make a long-distance phone call, each time casting a furtive glance toward the picture window and the alcoholic who was watching them through the lace curtains....

Coz was telling me about his idea for a new play. Marie was listening, too, until Uncle Sam called her over and started rattling on at her, speaking English at an entirely different speed from the Filipinos. Gracious where he was agitated, Marie was doing her best to calm him down.

Coz's latest plan, which actually seemed more suitable for a movie—I wondered if this film-oriented imagination of his formed the link between him and Asao's group—revolved around a jeepney, a kind of private bus that I'd seen myself on the streets of Manila. The main character, to be played by Coz, is a man who invests all his money in one of these highly decorated vehicles. The opening scene: Coz's village, in the valley where he was born and brought up. It all begins with the production of papier-mâché bears, a traditional Filipino handicraft, to be sold at the Munich Olympics. Before long this becomes an industry involving the whole village, making a small fortune for the man, in spite of the strong disapproval of an old woman who, having taught them how to make these things, is appalled at the way crude mass production keeps even children working late into the night. Nevertheless, the man loads his jeepney with the bears, and, using the passport and ticket given to him by a tall, blond, German woman, sets off for Munich to promote and sell his new product. When the games close, he travels from Frankfurt to Paris in his jeepney, finding various jobs along the way. At one point he is hired by a Filipino who has a commission for a vending machine that sells chewing gum, but for the most part he lives from day to day, just managing to get by.

In a letter forwarded to him via the office of Air France, he learns that the old woman has died. He and his jeepney are hired by an amusement park in Paris, and there one night he experiences something so fantastic he can't tell whether it's a dream or reality. He finds himself driving through a psychedelic maze, and finally reaches paradise, on a hill in the forest overlooking the village where he was born. The old woman and all the other people he thought were dead are there, alive, and the original wooden mold for the papier-mâché bears, passed down in the village for generations but discarded in favor of mass production for the

95

Olympics, has been carefully preserved. The old woman gets into the jeepney, and they soar through the air together....

Coz told us that in the amusement park scene in Paris, Melinda, one of his actresses—she looked like a teenager but had two children of her own, apparently—would be playing one of Hikari's compositions, on a psychedelic piano next to a deserted merry-go-round. The cooking had begun by that stage, and Melinda, her hands now free, was called over to play the "Blue Bird March," a piece Hikari wrote the year he entered the upper division of his school for the handicapped.

"That was wonderful, better than anything I could have imagined," Marie said, joining us after finally breaking away from Uncle Sam. "Melinda has her own way of interpreting it, though, doesn't she? The rhythm's different. I suppose Coz's village has a different rhythm too, but, listening to him, didn't it remind you of where you grew up, K?" Switching back into English for Coz's sake, she went on: "Remember the students' reaction to Uncle Sam's performance tonight—all the boos and catcalls? I thought it was a great success, but he seems really put out. He says the way he played it was meant as a criticism of himself as an American, for the benefit of a Filipino audience; he wasn't doing it to give the Japanese something to laugh at...."

"Here in Asia, the Japanese are the second Americans," Coz said.

"Yeah, but they're Japanese, they're not Americans." Blustering, Uncle Sam put his arm around Melinda's dark, sexy-looking shoulder.

"Seems like things might get a bit rough tonight," Marie whispered to me in Japanese. "It'd be smart to get away now. Our friends' cooking is red-hot, anyway ... I can't see how they can eat it and drink beer without getting diarrhea."

I had been planning to go home for dinner in any case; my house was less than ten minutes away from Sengawa. I thanked

Coz for telling me about his latest idea, and was standing in the doorway when Marie came to see me off.

"You know, hearing about that last scene in Coz's new play," she said, "where he climbs the hill in the forest in his jeepney and meets the dead members of his family? I thought, what if I were along, too, and Musan and Michio were there waiting for me; it gave me quite a jolt."

As I walked toward the main road, through the dark grove that still retained the atmosphere of a temple's grounds, I couldn't help glancing over at the spot where the drunk had been standing, but although it hadn't been long before, no one was there. I crossed the pedestrian bridge over the Keio Line and, making my way through the shopping district to the bus stop, past several narrow alleys lined with drinking places an alcoholic might have headed for, I thought of stopping to look for him, but then realized that even after reading all those letters from Satchan, I had never actually met him.

After performing on college campuses in four cities in Kyushu, the Cosmic Will headed back east, with stops in Hiroshima and Himeji. In towns where they hadn't been able to make arrangements with a university, outdoor performances were held in parks. In Kurayoshi, near the Sea of Japan, they built a makeshift stage like a vendor's stall in a park with lots of trees, including oaks, which were in full leaf. The city seemed to be keen on making its public toilets impressive structures, so Coz used the one in the park as a backdrop for the play, training the lights on it to make it look like a church. The rainy season had dragged on that year, so they had to go on stage with their umbrellas up. Uncle Sam stuck it out with one decorated with the stars and stripes in place of his top hat.

Before the Kurayoshi performance, the city's tourist bureau had invited them to the Ha-wai hot springs resort—Hawaii Hot Springs, Marie wrote in a letter. She had enclosed a picture of them all together in an outdoor bath, built on an embankment overlooking a lake. Judging from the quality of the shot, Asao already had the makings of a professional cameraman: Marie with her "wide-open" smile, cradled in Uncle Sam's long arms, half out of the water, her breasts showing; Coz, his hair and beard plastered down from the steam, looking very young and even smaller than usual; behind them, three Filipinos of a younger generation, standing on the edge, stark naked. A color photograph of the Cosmic Will with their Japanese patron, men and women bathing together—having a great time, wish you were here.

If this trip was keeping Marie's mind occupied, then Asao's scheme was working, and the atmosphere of the picture was cheerful enough to make me feel optimistic. But in her letter Marie said that at Kurayoshi, where they'd performed in the rain, the group had taken another bath together the morning they'd left Ha-wai Hot Springs, and although she had stayed out and watched, she was the one who had caught a cold. Also, that the Cosmic Will would be flying directly from Itami to Hokkaido, stopping to give performances in Aomori, Morioka, and Sendai on the way back, but she probably wouldn't be able to go with them. I could almost see Marie alone in Tokyo, sick with the flu, pacing in her bedroom late at night, talking to herself, and I gave my head a quick shake to get rid of the image....

On their return to Tokyo early in August, the group gave a farewell performance, incorporating some new details they'd added during the tour, at the women's university in Yokohama where Marie had taught. Melinda, who would be at the keyboard on stage playing Filipino songs, was planning to add one of Hikari's piano compositions to the program, so this time my wife set out with Marie in her car.

She arrived home late that night far more exhausted than simply watching a play could possibly have made her. She'd taken the train from Yokohama; Marie had been much too upset to drive. Asao had taken her home, but there was no telling whether she'd recovered or not....

It had all started with a newly added scene based on Coz's observations of life in Japan. In the monologue that opened the last act, he talked about how wealthy Japan has become. Why, there's nothing you can't find in the piles of trash on the streets. When he was a child, the village blacksmith used to pick through abandoned Japanese outposts in the jungle, looking for scrap metal he could use, but today there's no need to bother with stuff like that when you could even open a shop selling the latest high-tech electrical appliances; all you'd have to do is get up early and poke around in the trash. Look what he'd found just the other day—a wheelchair, with plenty of use still left in it!

The wheelchair was then hoisted up onto the stage, and the skit began. At that point, my wife already had a vague sense of foreboding, but what followed was sheer agony to watch. Two young Filipino actors appear, one as a boy in a wheelchair, the other as his retarded older brother. They're on their way to the cliff to commit suicide; this is revealed through their exchange with Coz, now in the role of a villager who seems more interested in chiding and taunting them than trying to stop them. "Our cliffs here in the Philippines are all knee deep in vines and under-growth—your wheels'll get caught and you'll be stuck there, chair and all." Though totally unsympathetic, he keeps on at them, refusing to let them go, apparently because he wants the wheel-chair.

Eventually they manage to break away and disappear into the jungle, the retarded boy pushing his younger brother. Enter a priest, played by Uncle Sam. A dialogue with the villager ensues. Suicide is against the will of god, the villager observes, so let's join forces and try to stop them. The priest, of course, is more than willing, but the other insists on one condition. Unlike the priest, his livelihood isn't guaranteed by the church, so it's only natural that he should be compensated for the labor involved in hacking a way through the jungle. Let the church take the two souls he's going to save, and he take the wheelchair. But the priest says he doesn't have the funds. . . .

In the middle of this discussion Melinda, playing a farm girl, suddenly emerges from the jungle pushing the wheelchair, which now has a dummy of a thin-looking wild pig sitting in it. Cheerfully she tells the other two: "Those boys have gone to heaven. I helped them, so they left me the wheelchair, and god gave me this pig as a reward!"

My wife told me afterward that, when he saw how shocked Marie was, Coz did all he could to comfort her. "He never dreamed she'd react that way, and it made him terribly upset. His whole body showed it; his face even looked a shade darker. But then when Marie'd left and I asked him why on earth he'd added a scene like that, he calmly said it was because the 'cosmic will' had told him to."

"I remember Coz saying he was planning to expand the present script and have it end with a scene in the forest, a reunion with the dead," I mentioned. "If characters like Musan and Michio were going to appear in that scene, wouldn't suicide be a necessary step on the way?. . . Marie must have felt she was being forced to watch what she'd dreaded seeing most, but Coz may actually have had a warm, sentimental sort of image in mind when he planned that bit."

"Maybe so, but the actor who played the handicapped child kept swaying and jerking around so much you could hear the wheelchair creak. I thought maybe it was to emphasize his being paralyzed from the waist down, but still. . . His arms looked awfully long, and he kept flailing them around, sometimes hitting the boy who was pushing him. The two of them seemed to be bickering in Tagalog the whole time. It made a big hit with a group of Filipino workers who'd come from a lodging house in Yokohama, but it reminded me of those old comedy routines one used to see, where they poked fun at people with deformities. When I asked Coz about it, he said the actors ad-libbed most of the dialogue in that part...."

A while later, I heard that Coz and his group had returned to the Philippines. Uncle Sam stayed on alone, though, and was still living in Marie's condo. He had asked a group of young Americans—some studying at university, others working for Japanese firms—to share the apartment, and they had all brought their own free lifestyles with them. It was Asao who told me this when I happened to run into him one day, but he and his friends seemed to be too busy winding up the Cosmic Will's Japan tour to be concerned. Besides, although they still considered themselves Marie's guardians, they seemed to have decided not to interfere in her private life unless she asked them to.

Then one morning, the first on which the chill of autumn was in the air, my wife, who had been reading the newspaper, let out a gasp; it was only a small article in the local news section, but she was shocked to see Marie's name there. At a Sengawa condominium owned by Marie Kuraki, an American resident of the same address, D.S., had attacked and seriously injured S.T., the owner's former husband, while the latter was trying to gain entrance. S.T. was already suffering from internal problems caused by heavy drinking, and a violent blow to the abdominal region had aggravated them. He had been taken to the emergency room of a hospital where he was now in critical condition. According to his statement, D.S. had been disgusted for some time now by the sight of S.T. continually loitering, drunk, in the vicinity and attempting to force Marie to resume her relationship with him. Local police had received reports of the alleged use of marijuana by D.S. and his associates, and were currently investigating the matter.

"Why do all these things keep happening to Marie, one after another?..." my wife sighed, the sadness lingering after she'd recovered from the initial shock. "When something like this comes along, though, you realize it's just the sort of thing you'd expect to happen to her. Still, it hurts just to think about it...."

"I think the English word 'vulnerability'—some anthropologist defines it as an 'attack-inducing quality'—applies to the state Marie's in right now. Even if the original incident couldn't have been foreseen, Marie's been vulnerable ever since, the wound still raw and exposed. That's how it seems to me, anyway."

"Those three bodyguards of hers will be going at it full tilt again, trying to patch things up, I suppose. You've got to give them credit for it, but it seems strange they don't do anything to prevent these disasters from happening. When they work so hard *after* they've happened.... I suppose that's normal for their generation, though—to keep a certain distance even from people they feel close to...."

"They may think that to some extent these things are necessary, if only as a distraction, to keep her mind off the other business. Because, as you say, there's nothing they won't do to help her afterward."

This time, Asao and his friends worked as hard for Marie as they ever had. Not only did they clear Uncle Sam from allegations of drug possession, but they also managed to help Marie settle her accounts in preparation for starting a new life; and, with that accomplished, Asao came to give me a report.

Satchan's liver had already been seriously damaged, and although the crisis was now past, he was still in the hospital. Marie had stayed at his bedside until he was out of danger, and paid all his hospital expenses herself. She had also decided to sell the Sengawa condo to pay off the debts incurred by the Cosmic Will's tour. What was left over would still be enough for her to live on. Anyway, she'd been talking lately about joining a small religious commune she'd found out about after leaving the study group at the Catholic church. As long as Satchan was being taken care of, that is....

"So even now, here in Japan, there are still people who sell everything they have and enter a convent, just like in the time of Balzac's novel," my wife said, to which Asao, carefully considering how much he should say, replied:

"Marie isn't actually going to 'enter a convent,' as an institution. I've the impression it's a cozy little group, gathered around a religious leader. She doesn't like pushing her ideas on other people, so she hasn't let us in on the details, but I'm pretty sure she's chosen something that suits her."

"You're good at putting yourselves in Marie's place, aren't you, you three? I really admire it. You never tell her not to do this or that...."

"We don't have that sort of power over her," Asao replied, and then turned to me. "K, you know how you sometimes use the word 'patron' in your novels? Well, Marie's been our 'patron' since we were students. She showed us so many different sides to life, in ways nobody else could have. That was an education in itself."

"And are you going to join the commune with her?" asked my wife, who seemed to be brooding about something.

"Why? What for?" Taken by surprise, Asao threw the question back at her. "As I just said, Marie doesn't want to influence us where religion's concerned, and, besides, she knows we've got work to do over here...."

They did have things to do over here; one of the purposes of Asao's visit that day was to ask me to write a recommendation, not so much for the Cosmic Will as for Coz, who was applying as an individual for a grant from the Japan Foundation. I had already heard the contents of Coz's proposal, but I asked Asao if he was sure Marie hadn't changed her mind since the incident in

Yokohama. This he confirmed: the play had definitely been an awful shock to her, but she apparently considered the question of helping Coz an entirely different matter. That was Marie's attitude toward almost everything.

| 7 |

A letter from Marie Kuraki:

I'm sure you've heard something about it from Asao by this time—that after giving up the Catholic study group, I've joined yet another religious group, or am about to. To tell the truth, though, I still have no clear idea of what "belief" is. Just the same vague illusions.

I have occasionally experienced emotional tremors I think might be close to "belief," usually when reading poetry. Yeats's "The Second Coming," for instance. When I read it aloud, line by line, I can feel all the hair on some inner skin (I'm not sure you'd call it the soul) stand on end. But this must be the sensation of approaching the magnetic field of "belief," rather than "belief" itself.

The poem starts with the gyre of time, spiraling outward. The falcon follows it, flying in circles, unable to hear the falconer's voice. I understand this metaphor originally comes from Dante, whose work you know so well. It's the descent into the abyss

105

of hell on the wings of Geryon:

> *As the falcon on the wing for many hours,*
> *having found no prey, and having seen no signal*
> *(so that his falconer sighs: "Oh, he falls already")*
> *descends, worn out, circling a hundred times*
> *(instead of swooping down), settling at some distance*
> *from his master, perched in anger and disdain, . . .*

I've heard that "The Second Coming" also has some connection with Blake's "The Mental Traveller," which perhaps brings it all the closer to you. The leader of the group I've joined (we call him Little Father) says that Yeats's poem is based on Christ's prophecy of the Second Coming in the Book of Matthew, and linked to the beast that will appear at the end of the world, described in Revelations. Little Father will be making frequent appearances in my letters from now on, but for starters let me just say he looks an awful lot like you—so much so that I laughed out loud the first time I saw him. He even sounds like you, maybe because you have the same bone structure. Honestly, if you were much thinner and didn't wear glasses, you could be his identical twin.

But to get back to the poem. The metaphor of the falcon no longer hearing the falconer means that human civilization has rejected the Word of Christ, and that the Second Coming prophesied in Revelations is drawing near. The opening lines describe a world in chaos, where everything falls apart because the center has lost its power; and then comes the line that gives me gooseflesh: "The blood-dimmed tide is loosed, and everywhere / The ceremony of innocence is drowned."

When we went down to the bottom of the cliff where Musan and Michio had fallen, we saw swirling pools still clouded with their blood. That was the aftermath, surely, of a ceremony of innocence destroyed. In a world where such things can happen,

*the best are bound to lose all conviction, while the worst are full
of passionate intensity....*

Yes, this is the age we're living in. From my own experience, I
can feel it to the marrow of my bones. And to anyone who says
that a paltry thing like personal experience doesn't mean anything, I want to say that I'm planning to do nothing but agonize
over what's happened to me until the day I die.

> *Surely some revelation is at hand;*
> *Surely the Second Coming is at hand.*
> *The Second Coming! Hardly are those words out*
> *When a vast image out of <u>Spiritus Mundi</u>*
> *Troubles my sight: somewhere in sands of the desert*
> *A shape with lion body and the head of a man,*
> *A gaze blank and pitiless as the sun,*
> *Is moving its slow thighs, while all about it*
> *Reel shadows of the indignant desert birds.*

This terrible thing, slouching toward Bethlehem, about to
come into the world.... The ending, too, pierces right to the
heart. A chain of images, leading from Bethlehem to the baby,
then on—out of the poem—to Musan and Michio, seems to sur-
round me like those shadows reeling in the desert....

This poem took hold of me long before I began living here at
the Center. (We're supposed to have as few personal possessions as
possible, but, even so, I keep a collection of Yeats's poetry next to
my Bible.) There have even been days when from morning to
night I felt I was trapped inside the echo of that cry "The Second
Coming!" Perhaps this is the basis of my "belief." The other
members are all about ten years younger than me, and this, too,
sets me apart from them.... But Little Father tells me not to let
it bother me.

"The Second Coming!" From out of <u>Spiritus Mundi</u>, where
all memory dating back to the birth of mankind is stored,

emerges a lion with the head of a man.... I know it sounds strange, but I feel as though I can <u>remember</u> that scene—through a certain atmosphere, or feeling, or something.... There's a photograph of me, taken at my grandfather's summer house in Komoro, the summer I was four or five. I'm in a grove of huge wych elms and tall, slender maples, out in front of the cottage. At home we used to call it "the lightning strikes picture." You can tell by the waves of flattened grass that a strong wind was blowing, and the dim light gives the whole scene a solemn cast. There I am, in my white dress with little gold clasps on the shoulders and red Mary Janes, struck dumb with terror. The shutter caught me with one foot off the ground, about to run to my grandfather who was holding the camera. My face is tiny, pinched with fear; the wind blows my long hair out around my head. A second later, lightning struck the wych elm behind me. Its trunk was left split and blackened for a long time afterward.

I can clearly remember the instant the photograph was taken. A gust of wind, filled with gathering rain, then the deafening crack; the shock threw me down on the lawn. For a split second, I remember being filled with a premonition—<u>something's going to happen, right now</u>—down to the very tips of my hair. I suppose I may have had some special power as a child, enabling me to sense when something extraordinary was about to happen. A minute before, I was squatting down picking flowers, with one hand on the tree to support myself. And then that awful dread, as though my chest was suddenly filled with the smell of blood. Without it I would have been burned to a cinder by that bolt of lightning, which split the wych elm from top to bottom. I would have lived on only in my family's memory, as a little girl dressed in white, and the world would have been spared a lot of suffering: not only Musan and Michio's deaths, but my own obsession with them, too.

The terror I felt in the front yard in Komoro, by the wych elm among the maples, seems linked somehow to this other feeling: that in some faraway desert there's a monster with a lion's body and the head of a man, stirring, beginning to move; even though I'm nowhere near Bethlehem, the rumbling in the earth makes my hair stand on end.... But let me say once again that I have _not_ embraced Christianity, I do _not_ believe in the Second Coming of Christ. It's just my way of reading Yeats's poem, I suppose....

Americans don't use the word "naive" in a good sense, but Little Father's teachings do have a certain naive power. My young friends here say that he can look at people and tell what message they need to hear just then, and at exactly what level. Also that to hear him talk, you'd never guess what a profound, rigorous thinker he really is.... So perhaps I'm the one that's naive. No, not perhaps—definitely. What I know for sure, though, is that he always talks at a level that even a new member like me can understand, while also making me feel, for the time being anyway, that what he's telling me is the very essence of his thought.

This is only a beginner's interpretation, but according to Little Father, god's creation of the universe is still going on. At the same time, the apocalypse has already begun. So although the world is now approaching the stage when the Last Judgment will occur, this is actually just one more link in the chain of creation that stretches back to time immemorial. I was right about Yeats's monster with a lion's body and a man's head—it's already begun moving its thighs in the pitiless glare of the desert sun. But thinking of it as just one part of the never-ending process of creation is somehow comforting.

I don't want to stand out here at the Center ... which doesn't mean I make any special effort not to, but I do avoid topics that the younger members aren't used to hearing about. And as long as Little Father doesn't mention it in one of his "sermons," they refrain from saying whatever pops into their heads about Musan *and Michio. So I don't talk much about Yeats's poem, not even to Little Father. At the Center, talking to Little Father means talking to everyone.*

Even surrounded by my new companions, though, I'm always thinking about those lines. It's the "rough beast" I keep coming back to: "And what rough beast, its hour come round at last, / Slouches towards Bethlehem to be born?" If it's taken to mean the Antichrist, then it's the major concern for Little Father, too, which makes me feel better about it.

As a scholar, he's only an amateur, but he's done a lot of research on the Antichrist, from a variety of angles, particularly the linguistic aspect. He tells me he's sent his inquiries out to specialists on return postcards, but has yet to receive a convincing reply. The "Anti-" of "Antichrist" has generally been taken to mean "against" or "in conflict with," but Little Father wants to know if anyone has ever interpreted the Greek Antikhristos as a neutral concept; as simply "one who came before Christ."

The trouble is, there's a very outspoken girl in our group called Miyo (she's Little Father's adopted daughter, in fact) who refuses to have any part of it. Every time the question comes up, she says, "But we already settled that in the study group, didn't we? 'Anti-' is 'against,' not 'before.' Why do you keep rehashing the same old thing, over and over again?"

Like Miyo, I believe that "Antichrist" is "against Christ," but, reading Yeats, I'm drawn to the image of that monster in the desert, slouching toward Bethlehem on its massive thighs, as a neutral harbinger of Christ, neither good nor evil.

Little Father is our leader—there's no doubt about that—but he's not a preacher. You can tell that from the way Miyo pokes fun at his version of Christianity. Here "sermons" belong to everyone, and we all take turns volunteering to give one whenever we feel like it. I'm the newest member, but I've already delivered several. The "sermons" are actually supposed to be

110

more for yourself than for your listeners. We're encouraged to listen to our own as many times as possible through headphones. Little Father records them for us on cassettes. In case you're interested, I'm enclosing one of mine. It's on "Dealing with Sexual Desire," and is the one "sermon" I've given so far that didn't bore anybody. Come to think of it, that tape of mine you listened to a while back (I was supposed to be playing a starring role on it, anyway) had something to do with sex, too, didn't it? I now realize how innocent I was back then. It wasn't all that long ago, but what's happened since has changed my life so completely, carved such a deep wound in me....

Of course, Little Father gives "sermons," too. They reveal to us the ideas that our life at the Center is based on, it seems to me. Responding to these ideas, each in our own way, frees us from our own lonely obsessions. As Miyo is always saying: "We're on our way to becoming blood relations, closer to each other than we are to our parents, brothers and sisters, teachers, or guardians."

One time, Little Father told us to imagine a very tall, thin cone, with a group of people linked together just as we are in a ring around the base. The "cosmic will" (no relation to Coz) is at the tip. Christ tried to bring it closer to us. In the very brief historical time of one man's life, he became its incarnation. But now the Second Coming is near, so we've got to hurry. He mumbled all through his "sermon," blushing as though he were terribly embarrassed. I can't believe he's actually had parents sue him for leading their daughters astray—he just doesn't have that kind of charisma.

Another "sermon" went like this: "The Second Coming isn't far off, and well ... I haven't got this worked out myself, but" (by this time his face was flushed a deep red) "though we're definitely not Christ"—at which point Miyo jeered: "What're you talking about? Of course we're not! Us? Christ? You've gotta be crazy!"—"but isn't it possible to think of ourselves as the

111

Antichrist? Not meaning against Christ, but that we're all pre-Christs?"

It's just like him to reduce an important issue like this to the question of how the "Anti-" of <u>Antikhristos</u> should be interpreted, and then send postcards off to specialists in classical languages and be mystified when they don't answer. It makes him seem not quite there, in a lovable sort of way. But even though it's a big problem to him, I feel that for the rest of us it's a clue to something buried deeper in his mind, and although he's far from articulate, his "sermons" have at least sparked our interest in what's probably the core of his thought.

At any rate, since I want to go on being guided by his way of thinking, I've kept up the exercise we call meditation. The Second Coming is imminent, and the apocalypse has already begun. The world, created by the "cosmic will," is drawing to a close. Everything is linked together in that single process, from the time life was first formed until the present day. But as this world nears completion, the time we're living in increases in density. (Miyo once said that time is getting more and more "conc"—from orange juice concentrate—and now she's got everyone at the Center saying it.)

Little Father says that your ability to sense the density, or conc-ness, of time will determine how well you live as the world moves toward its end. And that's why we meditate here at the Center—to train ourselves to feel the density of time. The day will come, he says, when those who can feel the increasing density of "now" as we move toward the end of time will—perhaps by raising their voices, perhaps in silence—achieve a deep harmony. By then millions of Centers will have sprung up all over the globe, and on that day they will simultaneously join forces, accomplishing what has been beyond even the power of the Vatican to do. Together, humanity—we, the created—will send a clear response to the "cosmic will" which made our world and is now in the process of completing it through the apocalypse. Miyo says that people in every corner of the globe, linked by signals from a communications satellite, can just look straight up and yell "Amen!" at the same time. That way, no matter where the "cosmic will" happens to be, we'll be calling to it from every imaginable direction!

These people with the capacity to feel the density of time increasing more and more rapidly as we approach the end of time are regarded as a multitude of Antichrists, so I can see how important it is that the meaning of the prefix "Anti-," which seems to weigh on Little Father's mind, should be "before."

As I've already said, meditation is the system he devised to train us to sense the density of time. He doesn't appear to be the scholarly type, and he certainly isn't a man of action—now I'm sorry I went on that way about him looking just like you, only without glasses—but I do think he's the sort who concentrates on one thing and then works out a concrete system so that he can carry his thoughts about it even further. That's how he came to set up the Center. Simple it may be, but it's a place for us to medi-tate, to make us more sensitive to the conc-ness of time.

It would be ideal if one could feel that density just by living "now." And actually there are moments when this is possible, but most of the time you can't _make_ it happen, no matter how much you'd like to. Little Father's system is to take the moments in your life so far that have left the deepest impression and superim-pose them on time now. Not by remembering past events, but by making it so that "now," and another time that is not the present, and yet another, separate time, are all moving along side by side, like several parallel threads.... When you do this you can actu-ally feel the density of time now increasing—doubling, then tripling.... To help us with this visually, there are pictures of rainbows on the wall, in the general meeting room, and in the rooms where we sleep.

This system of meditation came to me quite naturally; in fact, it's the main reason I decided to move into the Center in the first place. After Izu, I could never get Musan and Michio out of my mind. Even when they slipped off to the side a bit, as soon as I noticed it they'd be right back there in the middle again. That was the worst part—Satchan said the same thing in his letters. Every day was agony. Knowing it would go on forever was exhausting, and as I sank deeper and deeper into despair, there were times when I could think of no other solution than suicide. But then if I were to kill myself (as I might have told you before), it would mean that all those images of Musan and Michio that lived on in this useless head of mine would be wiped out. Not only had I driven my children, in real life, to self-destruction, but now I'd be obliterating the last traces of them in my mind.... So, even though I was suffering like this, I couldn't kill myself.

That's what I was going through when Little Father gave me this advice: "You say that the terrible 'now' of the time just before and after the incident is always on your mind, right alongside this 'now.' Why not try superimposing one more 'now'—the time when your children were alive and happy—on the other two?"

Meditation is the system we use to achieve this. When he gave me individual guidance in how to go about it, he told me that I could actually make my memories of the incident work to my benefit. "If you can't drive away those bad memories," he said, "try doing the opposite: take them as they come, straight on. But not as a cause of remorse, of feeling you can never make up for what you've done. Train yourself to bring the incident back to life, and superimpose it on the time you're experiencing now. If you can do that, there'll be moments when a third 'now'—the time when you were living happily with Musan and Michio— will come naturally to the surface and overlap the other two. Don't let them slip away! Then you'll have <u>three</u> layers of experience."

I did just as Little Father told me. And it changed my life. Of course the agony of that other thing, as something I'm experiencing now, is as painful as ever, looming over everything I do here at the Center, but I have managed to add to it the time when my children and I were happy together. This gives me a real sense of the density of the present moment, which helps me understand, little by little, how time is getting thicker and thicker as we move toward the apocalypse. Not that I've really grasped it yet....

Every morning, I use little details, fragments of memory, to get myself into the right frame of mind. For instance, I'm in a room flooded with morning sunlight, with Musan, still a beautiful child without any signs of the "warp" of mental retardation, sitting beside me, the very picture of innocence, listening to music on FM radio. "Chopin," I say, and he repeats, "Nnpa!" "That was Beethoven," I tell him, and he gurgles "Bay-bay." In the crib nearby, Michio is putting together a Lego airplane bigger than his own head....

That "now"....

Or, Michio has brought a little girl home from kindergarten to play with. They're taking turns telling a story combining Little Red Riding Hood and The Three Bears. The girl likes the name "Furufuru-chan," so that's what they've decided to call Little Red Riding Hood. It's Michio's turn when they reach the part where "Furufuru-chan" and the three bears meet up, and he gets everything right, belting it out loud and clear, reproducing—in perfect picture-book language—the uproar "Furufuru-chan" creates when she wanders into the cottage in the forest.

When her turn comes, the little girl, who isn't at all the competitive sort, asks: "What comes next?" "Ask in a small voice!" Michio whispers. He knows I'm recording the story, and wants everything to be just so. Then Musan breaks in with: "Ask in a big voice!" Although he has a fine ear for music, he can't quite follow the younger children's conversation, but wants to join in anyway. Being a sweet-natured little girl, she tactfully says: "OK, I'll ask in a voice that's just right!"

That "now"....

By adding those "nows" to the "now" I'm living in, I make time denser, which is the whole purpose of the meditation system. Of course, all the while I'm bringing those other "nows" back to life, sitting happily watching my children, there's another one overshadowing them—the "now" of Izu. There's no getting rid of it, and I no longer try. But recently I've noticed that my mental picture of that other, dreaded "now" changes along with subtle shifts in my feelings during meditation. And the changes are gradually settling into two distinct shapes.

One involves the image that's been haunting me ever since: of Musan, his simple mind stuffed full of Michio's tales of the misery two handicapped children like themselves have to face in this world, doggedly going through with a plan he's convinced is right, and jumping off the cliff, his fingers stuck in his ears to shut out the voices calling to him from the ridge. And of Michio, first persuaded by their warnings to change his mind, then galvanized by Musan's example and pumping the wheelchair over the shoulder of the path....

When I lay these last few minutes of their lives on top of the present moment, time becomes as dense as it could possibly be, which makes the pain of going on living more intense than ever. As though driven by this accelerating anguish, I stick my fingers in my ears and mime jumping off a cliff; I lean forward in my chair, my body bent double, the muscles in my arms straining at imaginary wheels. That's what meditation is: experiencing "now" as condensed time. But the more successful I am, the greater the drain on me, body and soul. There are times when after meditation it's all I can do to push through the curtain outside my bunk and fall onto my bed.

I never considered telling the group about it in a "sermon" (I

116

*didn't even tell Little Father), but I decided this was "hell," experiencing Musan and Michio's last moments so vividly day after day in this fusion of time. And that instead of clouds of sulfuric acid, it was this condensed "now" that filled the air of "hell"....
I've written this in the past tense, but it's still going on here every day at the Center.*

And yet, though I never would have believed it possible, there have been times when I've thought of it all in terms of something corresponding to "heaven," the polar opposite of "hell." This is the other image that repeatedly appears during meditation.

In those weeks before it happened, without Satchan or I realizing what he was doing, Michio talked Musan into dying with him. Until now I was convinced he'd done it by dwelling on the bad side of life. But now I wonder if I mightn't have been wrong; in fact, I'm almost certain I was. For one thing, there were plenty of things in life that Musan enjoyed, like listening to music, or watching sumo wrestling on TV, or eating his favorite food. He must have known that although he was bigger and stronger than Michio, he wasn't as bright as him, but I can't believe he'd marked himself with the stigma of a "handicapped child." While he was in a special education class and then the school for the handicapped, presumably he sensed that he and his classmates were somehow different, but he never thought they were inferior. He saw them as interesting, admirable people, friends to be proud of.

So it would have been extremely difficult for Michio to convince his brother that this world was a dreadful place, full of pain and misery. Isn't it more likely, rather, that he enticed him with tales of the delights of the next world? A place where all children, retarded or confined to wheelchairs, would be free from any kind of prejudice. Where all the best things in life—music, sumo, good things to eat—would be theirs to enjoy. And while he was telling Musan about this wonderful place called "heaven," might not

Michio, too, have found himself believing in it?

As I tried to experience that moment when Musan and Michio set out toward perfect happiness in "heaven," laying time past over time present, a change seemed to come over me as well. And I found myself feeling: maybe this "heaven" really does exist, just as Michio described it.

Michio probably wasn't always convinced of the truth of what he was saying, but Musan, in his innocence, absorbed the message—one that for him had the power to make him shut out other words, those warnings from the adult world, and step into the void. This power: couldn't it have come from some actual truth in those words of Michio's, regardless of his intentions? And didn't those same words, once purified in Musan's heart, then return to his younger brother's heart? It's true that at the last minute, Michio, tempted by the voices calling from the ridge, put the brake of his wheelchair on, but, even then, didn't he too believe in the existence of "heaven," echoing back to him from Musan?

In that "now" and forever, just after they jumped, Michio, his heart now pure and sound, rolls along in his wheelchair as lightly as if it had wings, with Musan, cheerful and lovable as always, intent on pushing him.... This is the scene that came to me in meditation, and as I lingered over it, it struck me for the first time—the shock actually gave me gooseflesh—that there IS a god. Thinking back, I may have had a premonition of it, reading Flannery O'Connor. And it seems to me that this was my "mystery"....

Tape of "Dealing with Sexual Desire"

All week this business with Sachie has hardly given us a moment's peace. So I thought I'd try and figure out why it happened in the first place. Little Father said, "She's one of us, so you might as well tell it straight." And that's why I chose this straight-out sort of title.

Sachie finally ended up leaving the Center. Judging from what I've seen and heard since I came here, she put up a good fight when her parents tried to drag her away, and I was impressed with her courage. I could hardly stand it, watching those self-centered parents, and imagining how cold the home they wanted to take her back to must be. Now that she's there in that home, my heart goes out to her. I think we all feel that way.

Sachie didn't want to leave us. We all knew that. But as long as she stayed, no one could meditate in peace. Our patience finally snapped, and that's how it happened. Yet right up to the end we were afraid she might try to commit suicide. Someone had to play the hypocrite and see her safely home—to her, a bleak, unfriendly place—so I decided it might as well be me. And it was no fun, I can tell you.

From Kamakura to Mishima, Sachie and I sat side by side and talked. I remember once when I was on another long-distance train ride, I saw two women, one much older than the other but not quite old enough to be her mother, having what looked to me at the time like a very sticky conversation. It felt really strange, watching them. But I'm sure we gave the other passengers exactly the same impression yesterday. That happens sometimes, doesn't it?

You already know what Sachie talked to me about on the train. We all condemned what she did, but listening to the story again from her side, I thought if only the situation had been handled differently, something could have been done before it got completely out of hand. That feeling led me to choose the topic "Dealing with Sexual Desire" for my "sermon" today.

By letting herself get too involved with Little Father, Sachie made a real nuisance of herself. Things came to a head when she started sneaking into his bedroom. In his own defense, Little

119

Father said he didn't want to aggravate the situation, that he only had sex with her to calm her down, but when he kept on meeting her demands, the problem got much worse. Sachie started saying she was going to marry him, and tried to boost her own position in the Center.

Now, even without it getting that far, if any one of us was given special treatment here it would have a bad effect on us all, and so we turned against her. The Center has always been a democracy; even Miyo gets equal treatment, and she's Little Father's adopted daughter. And since Little Father's a borderline diabetic anyway, another round of married life would be awfully rough on him [laughter]. As we all know, his main priorities are the management of the Center and the search for spiritual serenity. Even so, the commotion went on for a week, and finally ended with Sachie's being asked to leave.

But to get back to what she told me in the train. She'd had sexual relations with a boyfriend before she came here. One reason she joined us was that both families objected, and the relationship had reached a dead end. She found an answer to her problems in Little Father's "sermons," and decided to become an official member, so she definitely loved and respected him.

Not that she had any intention of sleeping with him at first. In fact, as a man, he didn't attract her at all. She thought of him more as an uncle, old enough to be her father—her Little Father [laughter]. But then again, there're no young men here at the Center, either. Sachie worked at a bar for a while, to earn money for our collective fund. But she was so afraid the rest of us would look down on her that she barely spoke to the customers, much less the guys she worked with.

As time went on, Sachie began to be influenced more by the powers below the waist than by what was in her head. Finally, one night she said to herself, "I've had it, I can't stand it any more!" And that's when she crept into Little Father's bedroom.

Once she'd slept with him, she began to be attracted to him in a different way. Whenever anyone openly showed her affection for Little Father—even Miyo—she'd get jealous and make some nasty remark. We all saw that happen, didn't we?

I think what Sachie told me is important, because this is something that could happen to any of us. I mean the head can lose control, and the powers below take over at any time. And when those powers explode, there's no telling who might head for Little Father's bedroom next. And he might just be in the mood, too [laughter].

So what should we do? Well, I warned you at the beginning I was going to be blunt, but we've got to depressurize that energy ("depressurization" is a word we used to use when I was in high school in New York). Masturbation is a handy way to do this. We're taught to think of it as morally objectionable, but it's only male onanists that the Bible condemns. And the object of criticism is the spilling of sperm onto barren ground, instead of using it to multiply the race, but this doesn't apply to us women.

And that's my main idea. But when I chose a heavy title like "Dealing with Sexual Desire" for my "sermon" today, what I really had in mind was our living conditions here at the Center. Because we sleep in bunk beds, not private rooms, if we want to depressurize ourselves it's unhealthy to have to worry about other people listening. If we're really going to concentrate on what we came here to do, especially meditation, we have to get rid of that kind of anxiety. So I'd like to suggest that we all masturbate freely whenever we feel the need, without fretting about what other people think. That way, hopefully, we can avoid saying "I've had it, I can't stand it any more," and letting the powers below the waist drive us out of bed in the middle of the night.

When things really get bad, why not masturbate to get your mind off it, temporarily, at least; I'd say it's healthier than turning to alcohol. I've never heard of masturbation dependency.

121

Come to think of it, you might find it among monkeys in a zoo, but not human beings.... If we depressurize, until the pressure builds up again anyway, we should all be able to concentrate on meditation.

8

The summer of the following year—the year I received Marie's letter and tape—I took Hikari to our cottage in the mountains of Kita-Karuizawa as soon as school was out. Our daughter and younger son both had club activities that kept them in Tokyo, so my wife stayed behind with them.

One chilly morning when a heavy mist lay in the air, refusing to clear, the phone rang. I'd woken Hikari up earlier to give him his morning dose of the medicine he takes to prevent epileptic fits, and was back in bed upstairs when I heard him pick up the receiver next to the fireplace. The cottage is a perfect square partitioned off into equal sections (the architect's concept), so no matter where you are the telephone sounds as though it's ringing right beside your ear. To escape this overly successful "acoustic unity," I've built a small study next door where I sleep alone when my wife and our younger children are here. After a while Hikari hung up. Judging from the tone of the conversation I decided it must have been his mother calling to make sure he'd taken his medicine, and left it at that.

Around noon, Hikari and I went out for lunch, down the path

with rank summer grass on either side, to the noodle shop in front of the old Kusakaru Railway Station. Surrounded by the rough-hewn logs of the newly renovated interior, we had our usual country noodles, and then went on to the supermarket, which was practically empty since it was still early in the season, to shop for supper. On the way back, Hikari, who had been lost in thought until then, suddenly broke his silence to say: "Musan's mama will be coming tonight, too."

If that was what this morning's phone call was about, we'd have to change our plans for dinner. We went back to the super-market, where I called Tokyo on a pay phone and asked my wife for more details. It seemed that, during the summer, all the spare rooms in the apartment in Kamakura that the Center was using were let to vacationers. Having lost the extra space they'd been renting at the off-season rate, the members were now living almost on top of each other, and with the other people partying all night long, they weren't sleeping very well either.

Asao and his friends, who had stopped off at the Center on the way down to the beach, contacted my wife to tell her they'd found Marie utterly exhausted. My wife suggested she take a break from the Center and go to Kita-Karuizawa for a rest, and this morning Marie herself had called to say they were coming....

We stocked up on meat and beer and went home, and had just finished cleaning the cottage when that familiar jeep of theirs pulled into our driveway. There's no sign out in front, but the driver obviously knew where he was going, so they must have stopped at the caretaker's office for directions.

When my son and I went out onto the front porch, Asao was unloading the jeep, while Marie quietly stood by. Wearing a big, floppy hat and sunglasses, she looked over at us and nodded, as though she didn't have the energy to do anything more. Her white skirt with accordion pleats and matching leather sandals had a light, elegant look that didn't seem to fit the atmosphere of communal life she'd described in her letter, with Little Father, somewhat past middle age, and his flock of young women, though....

When she finally came toward the veranda, following Asao who was carrying her suitcase, I saw that apart from the inevitable bright red Betty Boop lipstick her face was so pale she looked ill, although her expression was hidden behind the dark glasses.

"Come on inside," I said. "Would you like some cheese and beer?" The wide brim of her hat waved slowly from side to side.

"We had box lunches on the way," Asao answered for her, putting the suitcase down on the porch, then standing there looking embarrassed, staring down at his feet, as though he'd caught a whiff from under Marie's skirt as she slowly climbed the front steps.

"Asao's heading straight back. Tomorrow he's got to meet some people he'll be working for." Marie spoke for the first time, the strain showing in her voice.

My son had been standing quietly beside me, but something had been weighing on his mind the whole time.

"What shall we do about the pool? The sky has cleared up now."

Beams of sunlight darted through the birch grove, and the clouds shone white above our heads. It was the season for sudden showers, but on days when it had cleared up by the afternoon we went to a swimming pool about three kilometers away and had dinner there. Sensing that all was not well with Marie, my son must have been afraid that once we were all inside, the trip to the pool—not only the swimming itself, but the meal he was looking forward to afterward—would be forgotten.

"Oh, Hikari, were you about to go swimming?" Marie replied, quickly picking up the situation. "Then why don't we all go? Asao can drop us off on his way."

"But you must be tired. Why don't you take a nap?"

"I can sleep while I'm sunbathing. I brought my swimsuit," she said, perking up a bit.

Twenty minutes later we were there. After dunking his bulky body in the children's pool, Hikari was soon swimming in his own way, walking in the water on his knees. We had the main pool almost to ourselves, thanks to the morning mist and the fact that it was still early in the season. I went in for a dip, and got out on the side that overlooked a broad valley.

Against the background of a slope of glossy young leaves, in clear air that showed everything too vividly, Marie lay fast asleep on a plastic lounge chair, her sunglasses still on, her breathing deep and even. Her thighs, slim but with clearly defined muscles, curved like spoons along the blue and white stripes of her bathing suit, then joined the sunken valley of her belly like the legs of a detachable doll. As I stood dripping at her feet, looking down at her, the mound of her pubic region, pressing the bathing suit into a tight square, seemed to rise to meet my gaze. In Mexico I had dreamed of the dark clump of hair waving softly beneath it.

I lay down on the chair next to her and looked up at the swiftly moving clouds and green mountains, bearing down on me from above. The shape and texture of Marie's thighs and belly, I felt, weren't those of someone raised in this country; they retained the mark of a puberty and youth spent in an American high school. I thought again of her voice, frank yet urgent, on the tape of that "sermon" called "Dealing with Sexual Desire"....

A mountain breeze, heavy with moisture, swept through the valley, and I raised my head to see the rain pelting down on the mountain across from us, suddenly cast in shadow. The shower would soon reach us. The local children, already out of the water, scurried around in confusion, their teeth chattering with the cold. I watched Hikari, left alone in the children's pool, still paddling around like a sluggish sea monster.

126

A cry suddenly came from Marie. It sounded heartrending.

I looked around to see her staring up at me, fear in her eyes, her upper body twisted toward me, the bulge of her breasts shifted over to one side.

"It's going to start raining soon," I said.

"… I only slept a little while, but I had a long dream," she told me, reaching for the towel folded at her feet with her hat on it, then sitting up on the side of the chair, covering her chest and stomach. "I was at my grandfather's summer place, on the other side of Mt. Asama. That mountain over there that's suddenly gone dark—that's not Asama, is it?"

"No, Asama's on the other side. That's Mt. Takatsunagi. It's dark because of the storm, so we ought to get going. I'll call Hikari."

As I walked around to the wading pool, raindrops, sparkling white in the remaining sunlight, began to spatter across the water, stinging my bare back. Surrounded in no time by a shower that looked likely to last for quite a while, we had a meal at the pool-side restaurant. This was just as well, for though I made supper later at the cottage, Marie was worn out by the steep uphill climb to get there, and went straight to bed in my study, not emerging until nearly noon the next day.

On our way home through the fresh smell of earth and grass after rain, Marie told me about her dream beside the pool. Although we slowed our pace for Hikari, whose handicap affects his legs, giving him a peculiar gait that wears his shoes down on one side, Marie was so tired she had to stop now and then to catch her breath. But she kept the story going.

"I haven't been to this area since my grandfather died, but today I saw Mt. Myogi and Asama, and do you remember that big wych elm by the river, on the way to the pool? And there was that same cool feeling in the air. As soon as I dozed off, there I was, a child back in Komoro. In the dream I'm beside the wych elm out front, playing by myself, picking flowers, putting twigs in the ants' path, like bridges. I'm wearing my white dress with the belt and gold clasps on the shoulders, and my red shoes are fastened with buttons on the side. They're new, and the heels are too high, so I feel awkward squatting down, unlike when I'm barefoot....

"My hands and eyes are still busy with leaves of grass, and flower stems, and twigs for the ants, but after a while something different starts going on in my head. As though a video camera hanging from a branch of the old tree, watching me crouching there (yet it's definitely my own eyes), is beginning to see what's going to happen only a few moments away.

"In three minutes' time, a great bolt of lightning will strike, splitting the rough trunk I've got one hand on as I place the twigs on the grass, burning and charring it.... The branches at the very top seem to be standing on end, electrified, and when my hair touches the gold clasps on my shoulders, sparks fly. The tree and I are both charged, responding to the huge thundercloud overhead. Everything around me is entranced, waiting for the lightning to strike.

"That eye in the wych elm sees me, still crouching there, motionless, bearing the tension bravely for such a little girl, three minutes later. My hand's still planted firmly on the rough, scaly bark, when the flash of lightning, before I even hear any thunder, splits me in half and burns me to a cinder, together with the tree, three minutes later....

"In reality, I ran to the veranda, dizzy and staggering, to be held in the arms of my grandfather, who was taking the picture, but in the dream this is something that's still to happen, and with the perfect clarity of a mind in a dream, I know I can choose *either* of these three-minutes-later. So which do I choose?

"If I stay there, squatting by the tree, I'll disappear off the face of the earth, leaving just that final image of a cute little girl in my grandfather's camera. And I know that's long enough to live. Any longer and everything'll be the same: I'll grow up, have Musan and Michio, put them through their ordeal and finally kill them, then make their father drink himself to death.... I'm perfectly aware that's all there is to come.

"But the poor little girl in the dream, with better than average reflexes, jumps up, turns her back on the tree, and starts running toward her grandfather, standing there with his camera at the ready.... 'Why choose that one, so full of useless sorrow?' I/the video camera moaned, and the sound of my own voice woke me up."

When Marie got up the next day, so late Hikari had begun to worry about her, she announced without the slightest embarrassment that she was going to Karuizawa Station to meet Uncle Sam, who would be arriving that evening. Completely recovered from her fatigue and not as depressed as she had been, she went on to explain, oblivious to what I might think, that when Asao had stopped off at the Center and they were making arrangements for her to come here, she'd phoned Uncle Sam and asked him to join her, but he'd had something else to do at the time. She was planning to take Hikari along and catch the bus from Kusatsu that stopped in the village on the way to Karuizawa. And since Uncle Sam wasn't sure which express he'd be taking, if he wasn't at the station she'd leave a note for him on the message board and then come back along the old Karuizawa road, where she and Hikari could listen to some music at a coffee shop, and do the shopping for dinner, which she'd be cooking tonight.

Hikari, who can catch the drift of a conversation quite well as long as his own name is mentioned in it, asked, "In Karuizawa, what will the music be?" He was already looking forward to the trip into town. Thus Marie soon cleared the air of the small cloud of ill feeling she'd created between us by inviting Uncle Sam without telling me. Talking over a reheated portion of the Chinese meal I'd made the night before (stir-fried mountain vegetables with meat), she added:

"To tell the truth, the reason I asked Uncle Sam to come is directly connected to the theme of my 'sermon.' Sorry, this must sound a bit crude to you, enjoying the quiet life here with Hikari."

"That's all right.... We'll sleep in my study tonight, and turn the cottage over to you. Go ahead, 'do it'—it's all yours."

"Oh, I don't think we'll be *doing* it that much," she replied, drawing her jet-black eyebrows into a frown. But the next moment those red Betty Boop lips spread into a smile of pure joy which, I must confess, gave me quite a jolt....

There was something else concerning Uncle Sam that Marie had to tell me about. After we'd finished our meal—breakfast to her, lunch to Hikari and me—she went on talking from the kitchen, where she was washing the dishes, while I sat behind her at the kitchen table. As she briskly turned her head toward me, I noted how wiry her neck looked from the back.

"I'm beginning to have some trouble with Uncle Sam. I was hoping I could discuss it with you, so I talked it over with your wife first and then thought of asking him up here to the cottage. As I said before, that's not the only reason, though.

"When I joined the Center, for some reason Uncle Sam got very upset. Not that I'm expecting him to barge in one day and attack Little Father or anything, but if he does make trouble, it'll be hard for the Center to stay on in that apartment. That's what has me worried.

"Uncle Sam doesn't mean any harm. He's just a healthy American boy who firmly believes that if my"—remembering that my son was there too, listening to some music on FM radio, Marie came over and crouched down near me with her bottom flat against the wall—"that if he can satisfy me in that way, he'll have given me enough reason to go on living. There's also the problem of my soul, but he's never considered that. He's suspicious of the Center; thinks that if someone like me would join, they must be mixed up with some kind of occult sexual stuff. When, in fact, as you can pretty much tell from that business with Sachie, Little Father's sex drive is fairly ordinary....

"But I'm planning to go on seeing Uncle Sam, as long as I have the time and the inclination. Then I can go back refreshed, in body and mind. Anyway, do you think you could explain to him that the Center is the mainstay of my life right now? If I try to tell him myself I'm afraid he'll get angry, and accuse me of using my spiritual problems as an excuse to get rid of him. And besides, I really hate talking about myself that way. Uncle Sam's on leave from the master's program at Berkeley, so basically he's an intellectual type. He's just obsessed with sex at the moment...."

The urgent look on Marie's face when she was finished with the dishes made it impossible to turn what she'd said into a joke. We didn't talk much after that. We didn't have time; the bus came only once every hour, and since they were planning to stop off in Asama to see the sulfur rocks of Oni-oshi-dashi, Marie took Hikari and left right away.

I waited until dark, but there was no phone call. Worried about them in the pitch dark, on a path with no streetlights and very few houses, I decided to go down to the bus stop to meet them. On the way, I saw a group of three coming toward me, using their one flashlight to good purpose, and sure enough it was them. Hikari had been acting as their guide. Watching Uncle Sam carefully shepherding the other two along as they walked through the darkness, I had a new impression of him. I had written him off as one of the irresponsible new generation of American youth, but if he was in graduate school, he had probably had some military training back in the States.

Although all I got from him was a sullen greeting, Uncle Sam had apparently been chatting amiably with Hikari the whole time.

An avid fan of foreign language programs on TV, Hikari can carry on a simple conversation in English, pronouncing the words correctly. Of course, whether he makes himself understood depends on how willing the other person is to listen....

Marie told me that they'd found Uncle Sam right away, and that after finishing their shopping they'd dropped in to a coffee shop, then gone on to a Chinese restaurant. They had brought me a take-out order of spring rolls. When we got back to the cottage, I retreated with Hikari to my study, taking the food with me for my supper.

Within an hour, even with the heavy wooden rain shutters closed, we could hear Marie moaning, which I found disturbing. When we were ready to sleep, Hikari in bed, me on a mat on the floor, they started up again, and in the semidarkness (I'd left the bathroom light on, with the door half open) I could see the dubious look on Hikari's face as he lay there, still awake, his hands over his ears with the fingers spread out.

After giving him his medicine the next morning, I thought I'd go back to sleep to give them more time, but then the moaning began all over again, and eventually Hikari, still in bed, mumbled to himself, "I wonder what's wrong with Marie?"

All through our late breakfast that morning, Marie was smiling slightly with her eyes cast down, embarrassed but thoroughly enjoying it. Then, with the light step of a young woman, transformed from the weary person of the past two days, she set off for the pool with Hikari. I was left face to face with Uncle Sam, who sat on the windowsill, his eyes behind dark glasses with metal frames, his lips and nose (awfully cute when he was a little boy, no doubt) looking very pink for some reason. Marie had entrusted me with the job of making him understand how she felt about her present situation and near future.

Uncle Sam would, rightly, be offended to hear me say this, but on occasional gusts of wind that made the young leaves outside sparkle in the sunshine, I caught a whiff of something not unlike the odor of a male (or female?) cat in season as I sat facing him at the kitchen table.

Even with a delicate topic like that, I find that in spite of the effort it takes to put together English sentences from the limited vocabulary I have, things that would be hard to say in Japanese slip out so easily it surprises even me. This, mysteriously, seems to occur whenever I speak a foreign language.

"Marie enjoys having sexual relations with you, but she needs to keep working at the spiritual side of her life as well. So she can't leave the Center and live with you. Please try to understand her feelings on this point."

With every muscle in his white neck taut, the downy hair on it transparent in the light reflecting off the trees outside, Uncle Sam sat stock-still, looking at me with open defiance and resentment. I knew Marie had told him I had something important to say after she left, and to listen carefully. He was silent for a while, then asked in a deep, full voice:

"Why does she need a religious commune like that? It's not recognized by any church I've ever heard of." He seemed convinced she was hiding something from him.

"Marie needs that commune because she has experienced what is probably the greatest tragedy imaginable. She hasn't recovered from it yet. She never may, as long as she lives. . . . Do you remember that scene in the Cosmic Will's performance with two young Filipino actors? It caused Marie a great deal of pain."

"You mean Tommy and Jimmy's skit? Was that connected with something that happened in Marie's own life? I could see she was really shocked, so I asked her about it, but she wouldn't say."

Carefully watching his reaction, I told him how Musan and Michio had died. When he'd said he knew nothing about it I wasn't sure whether to believe him or not, but now I realized he hadn't the faintest idea what had actually happened. When Marie and Coz were discussing the incident, he had been standing nearby with the two young actors, listening; but apparently the story had seemed so incredible at the time that he'd thought it was based on an episode from some kabuki drama. That's why he hadn't objected to it on stage: it had just looked like a bit of black humor to him. And when Tommy and Jimmy had put on that manic act, he assumed it was the way they seemed to be sending up one of Japan's cultural traditions that had upset Marie.

That, I thought, is how it *would* look to a boy like Uncle Sam, from a typical American middle-class background. At the time of the drug scare a while back, he was the only one who'd been innocent; and now his innocence had made him blind not only to the fact that gruesome events like this really do happen in families, but to the kind of temperament that can turn them into comedy and laugh them away as well....

Uncle Sam's eyes filled with tears, and his face grew as red as a child's when smacked for no good reason, making his lankiness all the more evident. He shook his head, lightly enough to keep the tears from falling, and went into the room where the futon was still laid out, closing the sliding door behind him. He was apparently lying down, though almost too quietly for someone so big. I then heard deep, muffled sobs, like the sound in a dog's throat when it yawns and stretches. My talk had been *too* effective; feeling almost disappointed, I retired to my study.

Marie and Hikari had a good swim and still arrived home before dark. I looked up from my desk to see them coming up the path, singing a children's song from a TV program, their voices reedy but perfectly in tune, just as Uncle Sam was emerging from the woods on his way to meet them. Later, when they went to the supermarket to shop for dinner, he was there again to escort them. And during the meal he showed what a well brought up young man he was, serving Marie at table, saying very little, drinking one can of beer and declining my offer of whiskey to follow it. His manner was very solemn throughout.

That night, too, the lights in the cottage went out early, and as I listened again to Marie moaning, a strange idea occurred to me. The cassette tape the man from the television station had sent her—could that have been Marie's voice after all, distorted by the recording conditions? Perhaps the real reason he'd given up so easily when we dismissed the tape as a fake was that, at a deeper level than just sexual passion, he genuinely loved her in a way....

It rained the next day. Uncle Sam said he didn't want to be the only foreigner on a bus full of Japanese, so Marie gave him the taxi fare and went as far as the supermarket to see him off. The chill stayed in the air, so I built a fire in the fireplace with the logs I'd cut the summer before. Marie trudged back through the rain and, after taking her wet pantyhose off, sat close to the fire with her skirt pulled up to her knees.

Every summer I read an illustrated volume of the selected works of Brantôme, recommended to me by a professor now long dead. Not having studied the language formally since I graduated from university, my French is such that even with an annotated edition it's all I can do to get through a page a day; yet even so, as I continue to read, the easygoing tempo of the style settles comfortably into my daily routine at the cottage. That afternoon I was in the living room, putting the book down on top of the stove now and then to look up a word in the dictionary, when Marie, who had been watching the flames race along the quick-burning white birch branches, broke the silence.

"Wasn't there a passage in *La Vie des dames galantes* where a nun who was gang-raped by a troop of Saracens looks back and says she'd wanted to 'do it' just once till she was really satisfied?"

"That's right, I remember reading it in translation when I was in my late teens," I replied, swallowing the words "What I'm reading now is different, more along the lines of Brantôme the serious historian." Marie's tone echoed her own sexual satisfaction, and yet had a sad earnestness about it too.

Away from the fireplace, over by the window, one step up from where we were, Hikari was lying on the floor listening to FM radio as usual, but started to put the headphones on when he heard us talking. Marie told him not to; it would be bad for his ears to listen like that for any length of time. He followed her advice, but turned the volume down.

Marie thanked him. "That's Schubert's *Arpeggione Sonata*, isn't it? Who's playing it?"

"Galway, on the flute."

"It's lovely; it fits my mood right now as well." She turned her eyes back to the logs in the fireplace. "Little Father and I had an argument a while back," she said, beginning to unburden herself of things that had been piling up in her mind before she came. "It dragged on, and I felt stuck. It all started when he gave one of his rare 'sermons' dealing directly with Christianity, called 'That Which Can Be Sensed and That Which Can Be Understood.' In other words, the 'sensible' and the 'intelligible.' According to Little Father, anything that can be sensed can also be understood. Because in the beginning there was Logos—'that which can be understood'—and everything in this world, meaning 'that which can be sensed,' grew out of it.

"But in my children's case, their death was the worst thing imaginable that can be sensed, and yet I'll never be able to understand it. When I told Little Father this, he said that way of thinking was like Manichaean dualism; that the Manichaeans believed the 'sensible,' which is temporal, and the 'intelligible,' which is timeless, were in direct opposition.

"I said that was exactly what I believed, which made him furious. He started screeching like a child: 'Then what about the

136

Incarnation? Didn't the timeless become one with the temporal in this world through god's incarnation as Jesus Christ? And wasn't that what made it possible for mankind to find the path to salvation?...'

"I remember what O'Connor had to say about Manichaean dualism. The Manichaeans draw a clear division between the spirit and the flesh, so they try to approach the hidden mysteries of the spirit without using material things as a medium. In the case of the novel, however, the material world is used as a medium; that's what makes it an incarnational art. I found that pretty convincing when I read it.

"O'Connor firmly believed that what can be sensed can also be understood, just as Little Father says, and that it was through Christ's incarnation that this first became a tangible reality. She wrote stories about grotesque people and the horrible things that happen to them ... and made them into incarnational art, by showing that through the Incarnation these things at last become 'intelligible.' It's the same process as a mathematical proof; she begins by presenting things that can be sensed but seem almost impossible to understand, and shows that they can be understood after all.

"It's not novels I'm talking about now, though—it's real life, where something that seems beyond all comprehension came crashing down on me. Musan and Michio's deaths were suddenly flung in my face, with no explanation. And, for the moment, the existence of Christ isn't real enough for me to be able to say with any confidence that this can ever in fact be understood."

"But wasn't Flannery O'Connor also suffering, in real life, from an incurable disease?" I said.

"Yes, she was," she acknowledged, as quick to agree with me as Hikari had been with her a few minutes before. "And that may be exactly where the difference lies, between her as a Christian and me as a Manichaean. I've thought about that myself. If I'm really a Manichaean, perhaps I should start acting like one, and draw a clear line between the spirit and the flesh. And for me, that means ...

"Up to now, I've been trying to find some spiritual peace, but what if I were to give all that up and lose myself in the pleasures of the flesh? Maybe that's the only way I'll ever be able to forget. Because even now I can keep those thoughts at bay while I'm having sex. It even seems as though when I make a conscious effort to remember what happened, in a masochistic way, my orgasms become all the more violent.

"Yesterday, when Uncle Sam was looking so gloomy after he'd heard about Musan and Michio from you, I made him a proposition. I was serious, too. I told him I was planning to devote myself to the way of the flesh—plunge straight in—and asked him if he'd join me, as my accomplice.... But then (this was after we'd done it once and were taking a break) he suddenly got quite puritanical and started going on about how sensual pleasure is only temporal, and can't be compared to spiritual salvation, which is timeless. Oh, well, he was brought up in a Christian home in the Midwest, so one shouldn't be too surprised.

"... Tomorrow I'm going back to the Center, but I know I'm not going to get any help from Little Father. He's convinced that all he has to do is drag out Christ's incarnation, like the old noble from Mito brandishing his seal, and I'll bow down before him.... Maybe I really am a Manichaean after all, or possibly an existentialist—that's a little out of date, though."

The fire was starting to look rather feeble, so I set about stoking it up. A huge pine tree had fallen down in an autumn typhoon three years before, and I had been chopping the trunk into logs about fifty centimeters long ever since, at a rate of one or two in half a day. Each one would burn for several days. The white birch branches, consumed so easily, were only kindling to get the big pine logs started. The one now in the fireplace had about two-thirds yet to burn; I rolled it over, poked it with the fire tongs, propped some new sticks against the side that had turned to black and glowing charcoal, and blew on it.

When the flames had caught I turned around to see Marie's panties, snug in the triangle between those spindle-shaped thighs beneath her skirt, looking immaculate. It seemed as if in those two nights they'd devoted to sex (bedroom sex, not Manichaean mysteries), all the rank, earthy aspects of the flesh had been transferred to Uncle Sam, leaving Marie only with the spiritual....

I must add, though, that when she realized where I was looking, rather than demurely pulling her legs together, she made a suggestion, with a smile on that gaudy but now tired and terribly sad Betty Boop face, that wasn't entirely spiritual ... but may not have been wholly of the flesh, either.

"I don't suppose I'll ever spend another night on my own with you. So shall we cheer ourselves up and 'do it,' just this once? You could sneak back here, after Hikari goes to sleep."

"... When I was much younger, there were two or three women I didn't 'do it' with, even though they propositioned me directly. I regretted it for a long time afterward, so then I went through a period when I decided I'd 'do it,' no matter what.... But now that I'm older, I look back and realize that whether I 'did it' or not, the memories are there all the same, so it didn't really make much difference."

"In other words, we don't really need to 'do it'.... Either way, I'm sure I'll have nice memories of tonight," she replied, looking more relieved than anything.

We asked Hikari to put on a new tape and turn the volume up, and spent the rest of the evening listening to music. I remember now that it was the *St. John Passion*, which we'd heard at that cathedral in Ichigaya with Musan and Hikari, and I'm sure my son had a definite reason for choosing it. No one went to bed until the piece was over, and by that time the pine log had been reduced to ashes....

The next day, when we saw Marie off at the bus stop, she said: "You're lucky to have Hikari. As I gathered from your letter from Mexico, he's a real companion, or maybe a medium." She then pressed those bright red lips together, as if to keep back what she was about to say next.

That morning she'd told me that, as the conflict between Little Father and herself suggested, the Center was approaching some sort of crisis. One of the weekly photo tabloids that were becoming popular then had sent some photographers, disguised as vacationers, to spy on the Center's apartment, and Little Father was getting nervous. The tabloids had blown up an incident involving him into a huge scandal once before, and he was afraid of a repeat performance. For some time now he'd had a vague plan of moving the Center to America, and now he was making a real effort to get it off the ground. It would be difficult to get visas, so steady full-time employment would be out of the question, but they were hoping to work part-time while continuing their communal life.

If Marie herself decided to go along with them, she wouldn't hesitate to donate some of the money she had left from selling the condo to pay for their plane tickets. But with the differences concerning "belief" between her and Little Father still unresolved, she wondered if she really should. Although everyone was depending on her knowledge of English to help them over there....

She hadn't asked for my opinion, but as I listened in silence I felt that she had already made up her own mind. To put it in Manichaean terms, only two days before, she had shifted the balance in favor of the flesh, trying to escape into that world with Uncle Sam as a partner, and had failed. What alternative did she have but to return to the side of the spirit, and set out with her companions from the Center?

And as it happened, after I returned to Tokyo, Marie called and asked me for letters of introduction to friends in places where I'd stayed in America and Mexico. Knowing I would have to mention something of what Marie had been through, I put off the task for some time; but I finally got around to it, and in October of that year the group left from Narita Airport, with my wife there to say good-bye.

There was one more reason why I thought it necessary for Marie to look to the spiritual side of things for a means of escape. The last night she spent at our cottage in the mountains, I had planned at first to have her sleep in my study, but since Hikari took the flashlight and headed in that direction as soon as the *St. John Passion* was over, I followed him. In the morning, I realized I'd forgotten his medicine, and went back to the main house to get it, thinking I'd have to wake Marie up in the process. But perhaps because she was still as casual in some ways as she'd always been—I also felt it might have been an indulgent gesture toward a middle-aged man who had trouble making up his mind—she had left the back door unlocked, so I went in that way.

In the last stages of sleep, on the verge of waking up, she must have been having a nightmare, for I was startled to hear her crying out in agony. This was a voice so full of pain and grief it made the moans she'd let out with Uncle Sam seem human by comparison, and made me feel certain that Marie's wounds would never be healed by any human power.

9

Marie Kuraki's life from then on became somewhat unreal for me. This was partly because the image of a mature woman slowly, painfully, rebuilding her everyday life was beyond the scope of my practical imagination. Also, because the Marie that lived on in my memory, as long as one didn't look too closely at her eyes where sorrow and fatigue had left their marks, was a carefree sort of person, always ready for a good time. That morning, for example, when I heard her cry out in her sleep, she had been as bright and cheerful as ever soon after she got up, with the usual Betty Boop smile on her face. And it was the same rather light and sexy image from that cartoon character's world that formed around whatever news I heard about her from friends in the States.

It was the middle of October, in dazzling California sunlight, when Marie appeared before the first of a wide variety of people who were to come into contact with her in North America. To those who saw her working at one of the sidewalk lunch stands that line Bancroft Avenue in front of the main gate of the Berkeley campus of the University of California, she looked—from a distance, at least—as though she hadn't a care in the world.

I myself had been on that campus several years earlier, as a research assistant. While I was there, I had run into M, an old friend of mine, at one of those same lunch stands. She had been in Berkeley for a long time, and was then acting as an adviser for a religious commune some young Americans and Japanese had built in the hills, on the margin of land between desert and forest. They'd put up a sign at the stand, MONO-NO-AWARE, and were selling fried noodles and teriyaki rice to raise funds for the commune. M had come to America with her first husband, a civilian employee at one of the American bases, whom she had then divorced to marry a Japanese who worked for a trading company; eventually finding herself alone again, she joined the commune, and had been there for quite some time.

Knowing that Marie and company wanted to settle in California first and see what prospects might open up there for their own religious activities, but that they had nothing they could really depend on, I had written M a letter of introduction. Her commune had been thriving while I was there, but had apparently gone into a slight decline. There were now a few empty buildings on the grounds, among them a log cabin some distance from the main part of the commune, which Marie's Center would be allowed to use for a small fee. The commune had also provided them with the camping car that would be their main means of transportation from then on. M was getting on in years, and not only had the authority that comes with age—the first thing she'd said when I met her that time in Berkeley was, "Gray hair on a woman you 'did it' with once long, long ago; now, that must be a shock!"—but was also, it seemed, married to the leader of the commune.

California skies are usually frighteningly clear, but sometimes, early in the morning, the girls of the Center would awake with a start, thinking a nuclear war must have started, to find the giant

143

English oak in front of the cabin, towering over white birches with smaller leaves than the Japanese variety, making enough noise for a whole forest as it rubbed its clumps of wet leaves together in a violent squall. Before noon the sky would be a brilliant blue again, as though the bottom had dropped out of it, and they would set out for their sidewalk stand to peddle the snacks they'd made, and learn how to get along with Americans.

With the American sycamores, sugar maples, and all the other kinds of maple showing their autumn colors, the mountain road offered a gorgeous display for Marie to drive the used camper through on her way down to the university town. A group of art students she'd become friendly with painted the old MONO-NO-AWARE sign over in red and white stripes—Marie's aesthetic sense doesn't change no matter where she is, I thought when I heard about this—and drew a cartoon of Betty Boop on it as a symbol of the stand's new manager (though its original name was retained)....

According to a letter from a former colleague at the university, Marie seemed gay and playful to those who watched her working at the stand on Bancroft Avenue that year, from autumn to winter. From Marie herself I received a photograph that seemed oddly out-of-season, considering it was already late autumn.

The name of a resort, three hours south of Berkeley by car, was written on the back, and the young couple in the picture with Marie were in swimsuits. The powerfully built black youth was the Berkeley football team's star player. He was stretched out in a canvas chair, below the horizon of the sea behind him. On his right, wearing a high-leg bathing suit (which we didn't have in Japan yet), was a black girl with extremely long, muscular thighs —and with the camera aimed right at the bulge of her upper thighs and lower belly, no less. On the other side of the football player, in a sleeveless blouse, her legs primly covered by a full, pleated skirt, Marie, age and fatigue showing under the harsh rays of the sun, was still flashing her winning smile.

At the end of the letter to my wife that came with the snapshot, she'd scrawled a note to me. "Dear K, since I gather from your novels that you have a thing about pubic hair on young women, I'm sending you this." To be honest, it gave me a start, but fortunately Marie wasn't the type to pursue personal matters like this any further. Then I looked again and there, sure enough, was a thick growth of curly hair at the groin, peeking out of the swimsuit like feathers.

But as I gazed at Marie's smiling face, what touched me to the quick was that (even if it was just the light playing tricks) her narrowed eyes looked like two pitch-black holes. One could almost see the way her own ambivalence was tearing her apart, while the boy, his long arm around her, let his fingers play at the gentle, unprotected curve of her waist. . . .

Marie was working hard five days a week selling light meals with the girls, and enjoying herself on the weekends with her new friends, taking trips to the beach or the redwood forest. Aside from that there was the life of meditation and "sermons" at the Center, in which she was, no doubt, playing an important part. This because Little Father, whose plan had been to travel around the country in the camper and spread the word among Japanese women who had obtained citizenship as war brides but were now divorced and supporting themselves, had fallen seriously ill as soon as preparations for the trip had begun.

Little Father had been suffering from tuberculosis for a long time; it was while he was fighting the disease, in fact, that he'd conceived his unique world view. Determined to abandon any scientific cure in order to release his own natural powers of recuperation, he had left the sanatorium. The lesion had healed while he was leading a religious life, and hadn't recurred until now.

He had his own diagnosis ready: the "cosmic power," which until now had worked to contain the disease, had acquired an activating force in this new environment. And since it was the "cosmic power" that had made him come here in the first place, he seemed unwilling to go against the natural progression of his illness. According to Marie's letter, his condition had already deteriorated to the point where it would be difficult to take him back to Japan.

Although he'd occasionally used both New and Old Testaments as texts for his "sermons" in Kamakura, Little Father never went to church. But at the California commune, from his bed in the log cabin surrounded by a forest of now bare trees, he expressed a wish none of his followers was prepared for. Weak and feverish, he suddenly announced that there was a church of the Swedenborg sect, in the old part of San Francisco, that he felt he had to see.

When they took him there, they parked the camper near the top of a steep hill. The walk up a short flight of stone steps and across a lawn, dark with the shadows of evergreens, left him gasping for breath, and he lay down on a wooden pew inside the small chapel and rested for nearly an hour. But after that he seemed to enter a state of meditation, the ritual he observed daily. This went on so long that his followers began to worry and gathered around him, and in a voice as faint as the buzzing of a mosquito, they heard his final message. How could he have been so arrogant, he asked them—he, who had neither the experience nor the conviction to lead? Bringing a group of girls to a place like this had been a terrible mistake. . . .

It was Marie who described the scene for me, but even at the end she didn't join in the clamor this provoked from those now pressing close around him in support, the young women who'd followed him all this way to the chapel on the hill. When they started weeping and wailing, she apparently left them and, led by her own curiosity, began exploring the building on her own. On finding that the leaflet explaining the origin of the church was illustrated with Blake's engravings, she later sent me a copy, as the novel I was then writing concerned this poet.

Looking back, Marie had an amazing ability to remain calm and rational in the midst of a crisis. This was shortly to become all the more evident, for a week after they visited the Swedenborg church, Little Father's condition became critical, and another week later, in the log cabin at the commune, he died. And with his death, a new danger emerged. An idea began to take hold of the group: that they should set their own souls free and follow him to heaven. I learned from M how Marie alone fought against this scheme, patiently arguing with them and keeping a constant watch on what they did, until she finally succeeded in averting a possible suicide pact that would have made the headlines.

Besides Marie, five girls had gone to America with Little Father. Among them was Sachie, who had been driven out of the Center when her sexual relationship with him had become disruptive. This was to be her last chance. Sachie had left home and stayed away for three years, but when she returned there, she seemed at first to be reconciled with her family. She had continued to practice meditation alone in her room, though, and to give "sermons" with her parents as a captive audience, until she'd finally begun to appear as a threat to the entire household. So when a letter from Little Father arrived, telling of his decision to go to America, neither her parents nor her married brother, who still lived at home, made any effort to stop her.

With the confidence she'd gained from winning her long family war, Sachie had poured all her energy into the group's activities in California, and after Little Father died, it was she who first had the idea of following his lead, and was the prime mover behind the suicide pact. The funeral was held in a grove on the commune grounds—during that difficult time, Marie had taken charge of practical matters involving the commune—and by the time it was over, only Miyo, the spirited youngster of the group, was still wavering; the other four's minds were made up.

Until then, while basically conforming to life in the Center, Marie had always seemed somehow aloof, but when Miyo had come asking for advice and told her of the plan, her attitude underwent a drastic change. She put everything she had into dissuading Sachie and the rest of them from doing anything. She also made every effort to keep the process private, and, as it turned out, this was very wise. For as Miyo later told me, if Marie had let the commune know and they had tried to help her talk the girls out of it, this would have been interpreted as persecution by another sect, and, after driving Marie away, the five of them would have left the log cabin for the desert or the sea, where they would have gone through with their original plan....

A "sermon" given by Marie in the log cabin

Sachie revealed something to us for the first time last night. She said that Little Father had told her—and her alone—that he wanted us to follow him after he died. That he was setting off for heaven first, as an intermediary. Apparently she heard this quite a while ago; she said she'd felt it was her mission to deliver his message, and that's why she hadn't given up after she was asked to leave that time, but waited patiently to be called back to the Center.

I won't go so far as to say that she made all this up. I simply can't prove that. I don't believe any of you can, either. While Sachie and Little Father were having their affair, he may, in fact, have told her something like that, when none of us were around. It could even be that he decided to have sex with her so he'd be able to leave this message behind. Sachie herself said it was her own longing that had led her to his bedroom, but it's just possible there was some prophetic scheme in the mind of the person who willingly let her in.

Little Father often talked to us about heaven. If he'd truly

148

despised his life here on earth as a man with a body, that would make him a Manichaean, though, and we all know how he felt about them.... But then again, it would be understandable for him to worry whether we, the followers he was leaving behind, would ever be able to redeem ourselves through Christ. He must've been especially concerned about me. And if this were true, it would be perfectly natural for him—ill as he was—to think of giving up his own life on earth and taking us to heaven with him.

However, there's something important we should all remember. Whenever Little Father talked about heaven, he always said that in order to go there you had to have a "true conversion." Especially for Little Father, that was the purpose of the meditation sessions at the Center. But in the end, did his "true conversion" come to him? Had it actually happened when his soul left his body?

During his last days, we all took turns staying by his side. If he had achieved a "true conversion" during that time, he would have revealed it to us in some way or other. In fact, telling us about it in a "sermon" should have become his final, most important task. So why did he remain silent? Can you imagine Little Father thinking to himself, 'Well, I've got there finally, so now I'm going to die. No need to worry about the Center any more. The girls will just have to suffer their way through to their own "true conversions"'...? It wouldn't be like him, would it, to die that way, without saying anything to anyone?

It hurts to have to say this, but I believe the point he finally reached was not a "true conversion." What he said at the Swedenborg church, "How could I have been so arrogant—I, who've neither the experience nor the conviction to lead? Bringing a group of girls to a place like this was a terrible mistake"—don't these, his last words, show us where he'd reached when he died? I'm being blunt as usual when I say this, but he died disap-

pointed: the experience that would have canceled out this last regret never came to him.

In connection with this problem of "true conversion," I've been thinking of the "sermon" Little Father gave here in California, just after he realized his tuberculosis had recurred. As you all remember, he talked about the Confessions *of St. Augustine. I have the book here—he left it to me as a keepsake. Let me read you this passage he underlined in red; it's the part he chose as the text for his "sermon":*

> *At Rome my arrival was marked by the scourge of physical sickness, and I was on the way to the underworld, bearing all the evils I had committed against you, against myself, and against others—sins both numerous and serious, in addition to the chain of original sin by which "in Adam we die." ... How could Christ deliver me from any of them if his cross was, as I had believed, a phantom? Insofar as the death of his flesh was in my opinion unreal, the death of my soul was real. And insofar as the death of his flesh was authentic, to that extent the life of my soul, which disbelieved that, was unauthentic.*

Little Father told us that, just as the askesis *—the scourge—of illness had been visited upon St. Augustine in that other world, that* regio disimilitudenis *of Rome, he too was now suffering in California. Then he went on to say—and this part's even more important—that if he could only bear up under his* askesis *until he found a way out of this "other world," he felt that a "true conversion" was within his reach. Even at the Swedenborg church, when his spirits were at their lowest ebb and he let all that remorse come out, I think he was probably still turning these words over and over in his mind, clinging to them as a last hope. Little Father put his trust in what would come after his bout of illness in California. Didn't he himself realize, as he lay there* *racked by fever, that without this suffering there would be no "true conversion" for him, and that that was why he'd got on a plane and come all the way to this "other world" in the first place?*

Even so—and this is what's so sad—Little Father physically didn't have the strength to get over his askesis. Here in this "other world," he lost his life before he could escape. Human beings are creatures of the flesh, so there's no way around it. We've got to accept it—he suffered and died here, without finding deliverance, his flesh gave way—we can't pretend not to see it. Since St. Augustine's days, there've been infinite numbers of people who, like Little Father, have gone down in defeat to the "scourge" of physical illness. If this wasn't true, askesis wouldn't be the real thing.

We musn't idealize his death. It's wrong to say that his soul has gone to heaven and is now waiting at the gates to guide our souls in, when we've got no reason to believe it. If we refuse to see the meaning of his death, won't it mean that we haven't taken his desire for a "true conversion" seriously, when that was what he spent his whole life striving for?

He longed for it, desperately. And in fact he almost achieved it, but his body let him down.... Isn't it our job now to remember him in sadness, as a man who tried so hard, yet failed?

As long as we're alive, we still have some hope of reaching a "true conversion," so what we've got to do now is work together to escape from California, our regio disimilitudenis. The grief and despair we feel now is the "scourge of physical sickness" in a different form. But we musn't let ourselves give way to it. If we survive and find a way out of here, we may in the end attain this "true conversion" for ourselves. Isn't that the goal Little Father was trying to lead us toward when he started the Center?

Honestly, dying is something you can do any time. Why be in such a hurry? When I first came to the Center, Miyo, who was

even more innocent then than she is now, had read about my
children in one of the weekly magazines, and asked me, "Why
didn't you die then?" She had the deepest sympathy for me, but
she simply couldn't understand. Well, I'll answer her question for
you now: I'm just taking my sweet old time. So why do you need
to rush toward death now?

This "sermon" was only the beginning; Marie went on arguing patiently with her companions, and eventually managed to
talk them around. M later described her behavior during this crisis as "like a mother hen raising a brood of chicks. Sometimes
she'd be out in the birch grove, walking around by herself, looking kind of depressed, but then if she caught wind of anything the
least bit strange going on in the cabin, she'd run right back again.
I still remember the clatter she made on the wooden porch. We all
wear moccasins around here, but she never gave up her high
heels...."

M told me frankly that up to that point Marie's reputation in
the commune hadn't been entirely favorable. After meeting the
football player and his girlfriend at the sidewalk stand on Bancroft Avenue, she apparently became involved in a "3P" relationship with them (this was still fairly new in Japan at the time).
She'd slept with other students, too; it seemed anyone would do.
She was even rumored to be a nymphomaniac. And, as the high
heels showed, she did little to accommodate herself to the commune's lifestyle.

But her valiant struggle after Little Father's death was enough
to completely alter the general feeling toward her there. It left
an especially strong impression on Sergio Matsuno, a Japanese-
Mexican who was staying at the commune as a guest at the time
—and who was soon to become inseparably linked to Marie's fate.

Marie herself, of course, must have been far too preoccupied to
notice the change in the commune's attitude toward her, much

less the affect she was having on Matsuno. First, there was the task of keeping the girls' spirits up. She had to keep a constant watch out for signs of a relapse into group hysteria, which might occur at any time. And, besides, she was busy with practical matters that had to be dealt with. Realizing that her new American friends couldn't be depended on for financial assistance, she contacted Asao and asked if he could raise some money for her in a hurry. This is how I first learned of the sudden death of the Center's leader and the ensuing problems.

The funds she needed were for plane tickets to send the girls back to Japan. Yet she wasn't the type to wait around doing nothing in that *regio disimilitudenis*, the forest in the California highlands, until Asao and his friends came up with the money. After talking to the people in the commune, bringing the mutual relationship to an amicable end—according to M, this included settling the debts they'd incurred until then—she loaded the whole group into the camper and drove away, leaving California behind. Reluctant to send the girls off to Japan right away—she hadn't much choice, in fact, without their air fare—Marie had decided to take them on a trip, modeled on the journey Little Father had envisioned before he died, to spread the Center's message across America.

Travel brought the girls, who had lost their leader, back to life. As the camper moved further and further away, they shared the thought that they were escaping from the danger zone that had killed Little Father, and along with it, no doubt, the comforting feeling that they were at last recovering.

On their way across the American continent, heading east, whenever they came upon an old town with a sense of history they would leave the highway, even if it meant going miles out of their way. There they would make a stop at the public cemetery and—although this was probably illegal—take some of Little Father's remains out of the Adidas sports bag they were using as a

153

funeral urn, and bury them at the foot of one of the old trees that surrounded the rows of weathered headstones. The girls worked hard at the digging, and when the hole was deep enough to prevent dogs from being able to smell what was underneath, carefully placed a fragment or two of bone at the bottom. Marie marked the site of each graveyard on a road map—practical and very detailed, in the American style—of that particular area.

"What're you doing that for, when we're never coming back to America, and won't ever visit his grave, either?" Miyo asked dubiously.

"It's the maps themselves that are important. When you get back to Japan, take them to a picture framer and have him piece them together into one big map. You'll see the way the different parts of Little Father's body cover the continent," Marie answered.

Marie drove the camper through Chicago, and then left the United States and entered Canada. They arrived in Toronto by ferry, but, after spending only a day in the city (just as they had in Chicago), continued their journey. I know they stopped at the Cave Lake Reserve—if I looked at a map I'd be able to tell exactly where it is, on a line between Toronto and Ottawa—because I have a polaroid snapshot of them, taken by an American tourist they got to know there, and a letter from Marie. Some of Little Father's remaining bones were probably buried beneath one of the sycamores, or perhaps a maple, or a weeping willow; all were stripped of their autumn foliage. The photo showed them standing around the camper, parked next to a huge tree at the edge of a forest, the girls looking thin and tired but fairly cheerful, as though they were on holiday.

Marie enclosed some "sweet grass" with her letter, a kind of reed the Indians gather in the wetlands during the short summer, then dry to use in their crafts, and its vanilla-like fragrance had permeated the paper. In mentioning that she'd made necklaces of this "sweet grass" for the girls, she probably intended to suggest the episode in the *Divine Comedy* where Dante has Virgil bind the Pilgrim's waist with a reed when he is escaping from hell.

According to the letter, which continued in a drier tone, Marie struck up a friendship with an American writer there who happened to be the same age as me, and talked to him—I can just imagine the rather blunt but quite natural way she spoke—over a dinner in the restaurant on the reserve, consisting of corn soup, wild rice, the local bread, and the meat of a deer he'd killed that day. It was traditional Indian fare, but the hunks of venison served up on their plates were too much for the girls to handle. Marie was the only one who found this kind of food to her liking.

The writer told her about how a huge corporation had moved into an Indian reservation in British Columbia. The woodlands the Indians had sold it were now devastated, and, along with them, the Indians' way of life. He was headed there now, to do some research on the problem. Would she care to join him? She'd seemed on the verge of accepting his offer, which made Miyo and the others nervous, but in the end decided she couldn't leave her companions stranded there. The writer had taken their picture before they left, and bought Marie a wooden broach, an Ojibway Indian carving.

One reason Marie wrote to me was that she rightly assumed I would be interested to hear about this person she'd encountered on her travels, a writer my own age who was concerned about the fate of the North American forests. I had, in fact, met him myself. And later, when she picked up Asao's letter with the money he sent her via the Japanese consul general in Toronto, she found that I had also made a contribution.

The camper's final stop was Niagara Falls (from the Canadian side), after which they returned to Toronto, where they parted. They would go their separate ways by plane this time; the five girls to Tokyo via Chicago, Marie, alone, to Mexico City.

When they came over with Asao and his friends to bring me up to date on things, the girls of the Center showed me their last photograph together. They are standing in front of the falls, but since it is already winter, the spray is a thick mist that covers the background (drops cling to the lens here and there), and all that can be seen of Niagara through it is a dark, gaping hole. The girls, dressed in Chinese padded coats (who knows where they got them), look like refugees as they stand there shivering, huddled together for warmth.

Marie is beside them, standing straight with her head held high, her coat open at the neck, and a big scarf held in place with the wooden broach. Looking as though they're about to be abandoned, or already have been, the girls are obviously unhappy. Marie's eyes, as always, are deep in shadow beneath the thick lashes, but her face—the features more prominent now that she's so thin —is full of life.

They chose Niagara Falls as their final destination because Little Father had been fascinated with the place even before they left Kamakura. The world, he said, was full of wonders like this that show us at a glance how insignificant we human beings are, and these are precisely the places where crowds of our Lilliputian race choose just to stand and gawk. Niagara Falls was one of the best examples. He wasn't being cynical, either, for he had been looking forward to meditating there.

The girls in the photograph stand anxiously in front of the abyss, wet from the mist, wrapped in their own sadness, while Marie alone has her chin up, as if to challenge the world.... I felt I was seeing how the Center's members, on the verge of parting, embodied Little Father's image of Niagara Falls, each in her own way.

They threw the last remaining bone, his Adam's apple, into the colossal basin of the waterfall. They tied it in a handkerchief with a heavy stone, but even so it was tossed up by the swift current and carried downstream, rather than sinking below the falls as they'd hoped.

It was when they were all on the elevator that goes down under the waterfall that they noticed that Miyo was missing. What if Miyo, who was so attached to Marie, had lost heart at the thought of having to leave her soon, and thrown herself in? Sachie immediately slipped back into the hysteria of those days in California, wailing that Miyo had gone on ahead by herself, leaving them all behind. Their cries, all four of them by now, were heartrending, and loud enough to be heard above the roar of the water, prompting an elderly American couple to ask an attendant to call the police. Marie calmed and comforted them as they went back up, and when they reached the top, Miyo was there waiting for them. She'd felt ill, and had been sitting on a bench by the entrance the whole time. Seeing Marie, she got up and ran to her.

It was more the wild look on Marie's face than her friends' distress that had made Miyo burst into tears and throw her arms around her older friend. That day when she came to see me, she said she hadn't even tried to tell Marie what she'd been thinking while she was waiting; she'd been sure that just by standing there, weeping in each other's arms—because Marie was crying too—they'd been linked together by some strong emotional current. But she was wrong. As soon as her tears dried, that Betty Boop look had returned to Marie's face as though nothing had happened, and later she'd seemed far too busy getting ready to put them on the plane to have any time for Miyo's personal problems....

|10|

M iyo's interpretation of Marie's sudden departure for
Mexico City was, I believe, warped by her personal
feelings. She had taken to Marie from the start, and in
California came to depend on her more and more, feeling there
was a special bond between them. And then after Marie had done
so much for them—driving them all the way across the country
in the camper—Miyo was sure that once they'd seen Niagara
Falls from the Canadian side (the highlight of the pilgrimage Little Father had planned), she would announce that she was coming back to Japan with them after all, to take over the Center as its
new Little Mother. But Marie had abandoned her, and she was
deeply hurt. Nevertheless, when added to what I was later to
learn—both from letters Marie herself wrote from Mexico and
information I received from Sergio Matsuno (also highly colored
by his preconceptions)—I feel this episode lends a new depth to
Marie's image.

"Marie was so heartless it shocked me sometimes," Miyo said.
"So when I think of those two poor children dying that way …
This is so brutal I don't want to say it, but I felt a mother's cruelty
in her—couldn't that have been partly why it happened?

"In a magazine I was reading in the plane on the way back there was a story about a bar hostess who'd run away and left her children alone in her apartment. There were three of them—the oldest was five—and they held on for ten days, but by the time the janitor found them, one had starved to death. When the police finally traced the mother, she told them she couldn't help it; just the thought of being able to sleep with a man again and she had to go after him. Isn't that why Marie went with that Mexican who was staying at the commune—because he offered her sex? He was in his mid-fifties, and seemed pretty greasy to me ... and this after she'd gone so far as to give us a talk on 'Dealing with Sexual Desire'...."

Referring directly to the question of sex, Sergio Matsuno had this to say:

"The way Marie lived while she was in Mexico reminded me of a nun, an old-style one, dressed in a rough habit. Once we started our work on the farm, there were plenty of young guys around, and considering how aggressive Mexican men in their prime can be, not to mention hot-blooded kids, if Marie had been the slightest bit loose, things would have got completely out of hand. It was because Marie had cut off all worldly desire, just like a nun, that our project succeeded. But, on the positive side, too, she made a huge contribution."

I myself have a third opinion, one that both Miyo and Sergio Matsuno might agree with. In a letter from Mexico City, Marie wrote:

> ... I've decided to go on from here to Sergio Matsuno's farm, but, thinking about it, I realize that I've actually just let things happen as usual. Matsuno was so persistent, and I didn't have any plans for the time being, so I let him talk me into it. This is the way I've always done things, but still, I also wanted proof that there's at least one thing I've decided by my own will. So, after

159

giving it a lot of thought, I've vowed never to have sex again, as long as I live. I don't know whom I'm making this vow to except myself, since I don't have a god to believe in.... Smoking and drinking have no attraction for me, and I couldn't think of anything else it would be painful to give up, so I've decided to swear off sex....

This was certainly Marie's way of doing things, but after flying directly to Mexico City, she didn't contact Matsuno immediately and go straight to work on his farm. Instead, she chose to begin her new life by exploring Mexico City on her own, prompted by memories of what I once told her about my brief stay there several years earlier. It seems to me that she was performing the old Japanese ritual of *kata-tagae*, changing directions in order to avoid ill fortune, seeking in this journey to the south an exodus from her *regio disimilitudenis*.

After selling the condominiums, she had donated some of the money to the Center for their trip to America, but kept plenty in reserve in case she might want to go off by herself. When the time came to send the girls back to Japan, she arranged for extra money to be sent from Tokyo, but didn't tear her hair out waiting for it to arrive. Perfectly willing to finance their cross-country pilgrimage herself, she wasn't foolish enough to let their air fare leave her penniless. So, having seen them safely off, Marie left for Mexico City alone, where she spent a few days recuperating (physically, at least) and seeing the sights. She even found herself a guide with a car, a Mexican college professor who had sat next to her on the plane, on his way home from an academic conference in Chicago....

The country as a whole had fascinated her ever since her high school days in New York, but she now had a new interest in Frida Kahlo, the painter who was married to Diego Rivera. A postcard of one of Kahlo's paintings that she'd seen on the mantelpiece above the fireplace in Kita-Karuizawa, among a collection of souvenirs I'd brought back from various trips, had been the spark. I remember discussing it with her in the evening after Uncle Sam had left.

The painting was *Henry Ford Hospital* (1932): of a hospital bed under a blue sky with a few clouds here and there and, far off in the distance, a building that looks like a factory. A naked woman with the thick black eyebrows of a mestizo lies on the bed, bleeding from the waist down. A thick red rope like an artery is sticking out of her left side; at the ends of the six strings that extend from it are a fetus with the umbilical cord still attached, a snail, an orchid, a female torso on a pedestal, a lathe, and a large pelvic bone....

Marie already knew the work of Rivera, the leader of the Mexican muralists during the 1920s; I now told her about the brilliant but just as tragic—at any rate, utterly unique—life of his rebellious partner. I got out a biography of Frida Kahlo that I happened to have at the cottage, and began to tell her the story of her life, but when I came to the accident Kahlo had when she was eighteen, riding home from school in a bus that collided with a tram, Marie stopped me and wanted to know more about it. Naturally I thought of Musan and Michio, but in the face of the steady stream of questions I got from Marie—"There's no stopping her," I remember saying to myself—I screwed up my courage and gave her a catalogue of the gruesome details.

The shock of the crash left Frida stark naked. A bag that one of the other passengers, an interior designer, was carrying burst, and Frida's body was covered with gold powder, drawing cries of "La bailarina, la bailarina!" from the crowd that came running up. Impaled at the pelvic region on one of the tram's handrails, she was unable to move. All her life she was to say that she had "lost her virginity" to the steel pipe that entered her left side and came out through her vagina. Her spine was fractured in three places in the small of her back, and her collarbone and third and fourth ribs were cracked. Her left arm was broken in eleven places, the right one dislocated and crushed, while her left shoulder was also thrown out of joint, and her pelvis ruptured in three places.

As we listened to the tape of the *St. John Passion*, Marie skimmed through the biography, stopping to gaze, spellbound, at *The Broken Column* (1944), a portrait of Frida naked to the waist, her torso ripped open from throat to belly, revealing a shattered Grecian column inside, her whole body pierced with nails: an expression of her constant pain. And again at a photograph of Frida late in life, a ribbon in her hair, lying in bed holding the mirror she used to see the faces of friends who came to see her.

"After an accident like that, to recover, and then have the courage to go on pouring all that pain—not just physical, but the wounds left in the heart—into paintings like this ... and to carry it off with such dignity and grace.... You pity her, and are awed by her heroism at the same time. What an incredible woman," she said.

The atmosphere of that part of Mexico City hasn't changed much since the time of the accident, and as Marie walked over the square's worn flagstones, she stooped down to touch the hollows between them where Frida's blood might have collected. She also stopped to look at Rivera's mural in the Hotel del Prado in front of Alameda Park, in which he painted Frida as a mature woman, standing behind a young boy, the artist himself. Hand in hand with Death, an elegant female figure at his side, the child Rivera stands with his eyes wide open, innocent yet all-seeing....

At the house where Frida and Rivera had lived together, she strolled through the courtyard, overgrown with the vines and broad green leaves so typical of Mexico, and down a colonnade covered with clusters of deep red bougainvillea. She then peered into the bedroom, cluttered with little ornaments, too many perhaps, but each one carefully chosen. Compared to Kahlo, who was determined to enjoy her private life to the full, willingly embracing a wound so deep it would never heal, Marie felt hopelessly frivolous and inadequate—this she later wrote in a letter to me.

Seeing how depressed she was on the way back, her guide, the professor of economics—a rich mama's boy, still a bachelor and much too fat—had comforted her in his thickly accented English, keeping one hand on the steering wheel while he groped for her breasts and between her thighs with the other....

Wasn't it the emotional effect of the Rivera house that finally led Marie to contact Sergio Matsuno—though the professor's advances probably got on her nerves as well—and decide to join his cooperative farm? She enclosed a postcard she'd bought there —a clearer version of the picture she'd seen at my cottage, of Frida lying in bed gazing at friends reflected in her hand mirror— when she wrote to tell me her impressions of the Rivera home, and that she would soon be heading for a farm in a village called Cacoyagua.

The Matsuno family was engaged in the manufacture and sale of Salsa Soya Méxicana (soy sauce produced in Mexico), a business Sergio's grandfather had started, using the Chinese character for "wheat," enclosed in a circle, as his trademark. Soon after the war, when travel abroad was no simple matter, Sergio had gone all the way to Tokushima, his grandfather's birthplace, to find a wife. She had since died, but during their married life he had relearned Japanese, which he still spoke fluently. With Japanese trading companies sending more and more employees to Mexico, and Mexican society beginning to show some interest in Japanese food, the family business in Guadalajara had grown steadily.

But ten years ago, a Japanese corporation had moved in, and Matsuno found himself in direct competition with their new soy sauce plant on the outskirts of Mexico City. While he wasn't ready to give up producing soy sauce, he'd decided he should do something else to compensate for his loss of business, and came up with the idea of starting a farm where he could grow flowers and vegetables, which he would then transport into Mexico City by truck.

A plot of land that the Matsuno family had owned since before the war, in the village of Cacoyagua, was chosen as the site for the farm. It had once been an isolated spot, accessible only by a narrow track that wound through valleys hemmed in by high mountains on either side, but now there was a paved road that stretched all the way into the hills, making it possible to reach Mexico City in four hours. About halfway down a steep slope that led to a rock-strewn desert below was a church, built with stones brought from the Aztec pyramid on the summit, and the village, a few houses clustered around it.

Further down, beside a ravine where a river flowed during the rainy season, was a level piece of land with a few willow trees growing on it. Once wells had been sunk to make sure water would be available in the dry season, the farm was built here. With the dream of developing it eventually into a workplace where young Indians, mestizos, and Japanese-Mexicans from the colony in Mexico City could live together and support themselves, Sergio Matsuno began his enterprise.

The rocky land was cleared and, according to plan, flowers and vegetables grown on the farm were soon making their way into the city, along the road that crossed the desert, climbed into the wooded highlands, and descended through another valley until it finally reached the densely populated urban area. Then the Mexican economy fell into a recession which continued for several years, plunging both the soy sauce factory and the farm into a crisis. Once again forced to take action, Matsuno decided to cut back on soy sauce production and turn the farm into a full cooperative.

Matsuno's grandfather, with an uncompromising pacifism rooted in his Christian beliefs, had come to Mexico to avoid being called up for military service in Japan, and the family had been active in the church for generations. Matsuno now donated the farm to the church in Cacoyagua and, on the strength of his religious connections, traveled to Hawaii and Japan to raise funds for what he planned to be a collective enterprise run by people sharing the same faith. He was particularly successful in Japan, with its strong currency.

On his way home, he stopped off at the commune in California. The people there had known him for some time, as customers of his Salsa Soya Méxicana, which was made without preservatives and in competition with international corporations. And it was there that he was introduced to Marie; in fact, it may have been Matsuno who gave her the idea of sending home for money to pay for the girls' air fare.

Now that he could see an end to his financial problems, Matsuno needed a person who could be a symbol for his farm, on the eve of its rebirth as a religious institution, to motivate his workers, especially the young Indians and mestizos. Of course they had the guidance of the priest. But he wanted someone from the secular world as well, a worker who would also be a figurehead they could unite around. It was this missing element in his plan that he was hoping to discuss with the leader of the commune while he was in California.... So when he was told the tragic story of Marie Kuraki, a guest from Japan then staying at the commune with a group called the Center, he immediately saw an answer to his problem. But rather than describe how he persuaded her to take on the role he had in mind, I'll leave it to a letter from Marie herself to show what happened:

> ... *Miyo and the other girls kept saying there was something dubious about the way Matsuno approached me. I'm sure they've*

told you what they think of him by this time. Actually they're right—there is something dubious about him. But then, I've always felt quite at home with people like that when they've come to me in the past. The fact that Matsuno makes no attempt to hide it from anyone may be what led me to think about joining his farm in Cacoyagua in the first place. He seems desperate, determined to believe in what you might call the "truth" that can come out of a "dubious" proposition. And for all his craftiness, you can tell he comes from a hardworking Christian family who've kept a business going for three generations and stopped on the Sabbath to pray.

This is how Matsuno is planning to introduce me to the people on his farm. I'm a mother who lost her children in a horrible way, but in their deaths I saw a "mystery".... And to put what I got from that experience to work in real life, I've come halfway across the globe, determined to serve god by working with them.... He'd like me to tell that to the people on the farm myself. But if I don't want to, that's all right; just seeing me working away quietly will be enough to convince them that what he's told them about me is true....

Matsuno is not only a bit dubious, he's shrewd. In Japan, he says, something like what happened in my family may get splashed all over the news every morning for a while, but it'll be forgotten all the more quickly because of it. Whereas on the farm in Mexico, once the story gets around, it'll be carved in people's memories as deeply as in stone, and the effect will go on and on....

A banner to unite under: that's what working with me would provide, a woman who has carved the "mystery" of her children's hideous deaths on her heart and dedicated her life to hard physical labor. They've never really been a group, the people on the farm, and without meaning to do anything wrong, they tend to goof off whenever they get the chance. So there you have it. And Matsuno has begun to show <u>me</u> *what this new life will be like as* well. No matter how I choose to live, I'll never escape from my children's deaths, so why not take up the burden of their memory again and, as I work, bear witness to it along with the people working beside me—wouldn't that be the most natural way for me to live?...

By this time I must have tried thinking about what happened to Musan and Michio from every possible angle. For instance, once when I was writing to you two, partly because K is a writer, I realized I was looking back at the event as though it were a novel, trying to interpret it in some new way.

And thinking further along these lines, Flannery O'Connor immediately came to mind. As I've said or written before, in O'Connor's case, once she's presented the tragedy, the novel is complete. And, in it, the "mystery" is expressed through the "manners" of everyday life. That comes through very clearly, even to someone like me, who doesn't have her religious faith. But when I presented what had happened in my own life in a novelistic form, the "mystery" simply didn't appear.

I told Sergio Matsuno that, but he just started right in on me again, finding a new angle in what I'd said. He suggested I think of it this way: "As one part of this world that god is in the process of creating, what happened to your children is 'intelligible'— why not <u>proclaim</u> that to the world? And while you're doing that, go one step further and offer your services willingly to the god who forced that experience on you....

"If you try doing this, as a mother, at least the people working with you every day will begin to see the 'mystery' of it, won't they? To the simple people on the farm in Cacoyagua, won't the outward appearance of that 'mystery' be revealed—as something separate from you, from your inner life?"

Needless to say, I told him I personally can't believe in tales of "mystery" like this. I'll never be able to see what happened to Musan and Michio as "intelligible." And I don't believe there's a

167

transcendent point of view to show me it is, either....

Matsuno listened carefully, then countered: "You keep saying you can't believe, that you feel you're hanging in midair. For you, no doubt, that's a big problem; but for the people in Cacoyagua, who'll just be seeing you from the outside, reading your story with their own eyes, it doesn't matter. You may still be confused inside, but if you—the mother—keep on proclaiming that your sons' awful death is 'intelligible,' and offer the sight of yourself working your heart out as a sign to prove it, that'll be enough to make the story complete for them.

"And what if," he went on, his eyes drawing me into what was about to come next, "as the days go by, filled with nothing but hard work—what if something you never expected happened in your own heart, hanging there stubbornly in midair? I mean, isn't it just possible that a 'mystery' might be revealed to you? And if that happened, if you were suddenly struck by that 'mystery,' wouldn't it be you more than anyone else—you who've had that disaster happen, and been caught in this awful uncertainty ever since, unable to get beyond it, suffering as you work —wouldn't it be you who'd understand suddenly that everything *is* 'intelligible'?"

And then one day, after I'd made up my mind to join the farm, Matsuno and I were strolling around the north side of Alameda Park—that hotel with the Rivera mural called <u>Dream of a Sunday Afternoon on the Alameda</u> is on the south side, remember?—walking off some tacos we'd eaten at a street stall. Having originally been at the bottom of lake, the whole of Mexico City is apparently sinking now, due to the drawing off of ground water, but as we strolled along we came across an old stone church that looked as though it had been submerged, listing to one side, since long before that started happening, and decided to go in for a look.

At a little shop near the entrance they were selling tiny golden

168

charms—legs, and arms, and eyes. Matsuno told me that people leave these trinkets as offerings on the altar when they pray for the corresponding part of the body to be healed. I admit I couldn't help thinking, for Musan I'd choose this head, and for Michio maybe this pair of legs, but I managed to walk on calmly by. But then, as we were going around the church, perhaps encouraged by the religious atmosphere—the dim light and everything—Matsuno suddenly came out with this:

"I know how painful it must've been for you, but when Musan and Michio killed themselves, don't you think god might have been revealed in the order in which they died? I don't want to push this point too hard since for you the whole thing is 'unintelligible'.... But if you're willing to listen, this is what I mean. It began with Michio slowly convincing Musan to go along with him, isn't that right? So if they'd died according to the original scheme, just as Michio planned it, no one could say god had entered into it at all. But at the crucial moment, his plan broke down, didn't it? Musan was supposed to push Michio's wheelchair over the cliff, but that idea was dropped. In other words, Musan lost his job of guiding Michio's wheelchair, which was to have led him into death. At that point, though, feeling useless, abandoned, didn't Musan hear god calling to him ... and, inspired by what he heard, choose to die in a way that was different from the plan Michio had carefully taught him? Then when he saw his brother jump, right before his eyes, didn't Michio see the way god had called him, and decide to die himself?... A 'mystery' was revealed right at that moment, don't you think?"

I was in a daze. It was dark inside the church, and the stone floor was so worn it curved like the bottom of a boat, which made it hard to walk on, so I was only some way down the aisle when I looked over and saw a very Mexican-looking portrait of the Virgin of Guadalupe hanging on the wall. She had her eyes cast down, as mestizo women often do, but I felt she was glanc-

169

ing at me. On the verge of bursting into tears and falling on my knees, I somehow got hold of myself and, taking courage, silently repeated: "NO! I WON'T! I WON'T!" as I headed for the door, made from wood as weatherbeaten as an old ship's timber, and pushed it open. I emerged into the startlingly clear, bracing air of twilight in Mexico City which, as K once said, seems to go on forever.

This was the last letter my wife and I received from Marie. Asao and his friends wouldn't contact me unless she specifically asked for our cooperation, so since the day they'd come over to let me know of the Center's safe return, I hadn't heard from them, either. When I remembered Marie from time to time, I now associated her face with the Mexican image of the Virgin Mary she mentioned in her letter. The figure of this Virgin, said to have appeared at Guadalupe, has traveled throughout the Mexican countryside to reach the local Indian population, and in the ancient convents you find tucked away in remote valleys, she almost always has the dark skin and features of an Indian woman.

The Virgin of Guadalupe, and Marie emerging into the twilight from the gloom inside the church as though rising to the earth's surface, exposing eyes like two holes deep in shadow, and bright red Betty Boop lips, to the chill air of late autumn. Once when I was talking to my wife about my memories of Marie, she commented: "You know, it's unusual for an adult to have such long, thick eyelashes. Those flimsy false ones you see women wearing are no match for hers." So there was a physical explanation (not that I hadn't noticed it myself) for the shadows that had always made her eyes look like black holes to me.

Over the following few years, I wondered why we hadn't heard from Marie for so long, and thought perhaps we should try to find out what was going on through Asao. But my wife was reluctant to do this; if the need arose, Marie would surely find a phone and make an overseas call, so wouldn't it be better just to wait, and be ready to help when she did?

"First she joins the Center in Kamakura, follows them to the commune in California, and then goes on to the farm in Mexico. Don't you think that deep down she wanted to get as far away from Tokyo as possible? After all, she could have come back from Toronto with the girls if she'd wanted to.... And that would mean she wanted to distance herself from the people she knows here, too, wouldn't it? So it's probably best not to chase after her, not try too hard to keep in touch.... You've been letting yourself get too involved with Marie lately, anyway. Maybe with her so far away your feelings will settle down a bit."

During those years, I broke my long-established habit of drinking myself into a stupor every night in order to get to sleep. The first year I didn't allow myself even a can of beer, and when I had trouble falling asleep—day after day I'd lie in bed awake in my study until the pair of turtledoves nesting in the mountain camellia outside the window started cooing to each other at dawn—I read novels, one after another, trying somehow to get through the night.

I read Dickens, and Balzac. When I happened to reread *Le Curé de village*, my thoughts were inevitably drawn to Marie's life in Mexico. I couldn't help merging Véronique's large-scale irrigation project with Marie's enterprise on the farm. Besides, the village that "la belle madame Graslin" saves is referred to in French as a *commune*, which made for another connection.

Véronique's eyes were always special—even before her beauty was restored and she knew she'd finally be able to atone for her sins. When she was excited the pupils grew large, the blue irises dwindling to a barely visible rim around them. Blue eyes turning dark. Véronique's final ecstasy gleamed in those dark eyes.

Marie certainly didn't believe her own sins were the sole cause of what had happened to her children. I was sure of that myself. I

171

also felt sure that the incident would always be an immovable obstacle in her heart. And yet, though she'd said in her letter she would never be able to accept their death as something "intelligible"—which I couldn't imagine her doing either—what if that impossibility actually came about, through her labor on the farm in Mexico? With this thought, despite my own inability to come to any rational conclusion about it, those bright Betty Boop features seemed to regain their radiance, looking just as they had at the time of the hunger strike in the Ginza, when Musan, though handicapped, was alive, and nothing irrevocable had happened yet....

So, as I imagined this scene, superimposing Marie onto Balzac's character, I was envisioning her final transformation; which means that before hearing of her fatal illness, I was thinking about her death—and for no real reason, I was simply letting my mind wander. But, looking back, there were a couple of memories that might have served as a catalyst.

I have already mentioned my visit to Malinalco, a village in a similar setting and at about the same distance from Mexico City as Cacoyagua, where Marie's farm was. We started from Mexico City by car, climbing first into the surrounding highlands, then dropping into the valley below. Without conflicting with the clear blue above our heads, a storm lowered like the sky in an El Greco painting over the next valley, while beyond it was another stretch of cloudless blue. Beneath this endless expanse of sky, the journey deep into valley after valley made me feel as though we were going down into the underworld. My Argentine assistant, who was driving, said: "When I reach this pass, I always remember the road through Plato's *regio dismultitudenis*." That's the first thing.

The other was something my wife had heard from Marie soon after she'd joined the Center, but hadn't told me about in detail as it involved the inner workings of the female body. Marie had had a lump in her breast and was worried it might be malignant, but thanks to meditation she couldn't feel it any longer with her fingers.... My wife had said she saw no reason to doubt Little Father's powers as a religious leader, but suggested Marie come with her to the clinic where she had her yearly checkup, to make sure it was really nothing to worry about. Some time before, when Marie had gone to the local doctor with a stubborn cold, he had recommended she have her thyroid gland checked, and she had seemed willing to take my wife up on her offer. But before an appointment could be made, Marie had left for America with her group.

As it turned out, of course, it wasn't until five years after Marie had joined the farm at Cacoyagua, when Sergio Matsuno came to tell me she was dying of cancer and to discuss the movie they were planning as a memorial of her life, that these vague associations took on the weight of reality....

| 11 |

Sergio Matsuno didn't come all the way to Japan just to tell me that Marie was dying of cancer in a hospital in Guadalajara. His father, who had been interned in a relocation center at the outbreak of World War II and then placed under house arrest in Mexico City, was now eighty-five, and after being decorated by the Japanese government the year before, was determined to celebrate the event with a trip back to Tokushima to visit the grave of his ancestors. Matsuno himself, despite having had a valid reason for cutting back on the family soy sauce business to concentrate on farming, felt guilty about it, and wanted to make it up to his father; so he'd decided to accompany the old man, even if it meant leaving Marie for a while.

Things being as they were, as long as he could be sure his father would survive the rigors of the round-trip flight, Matsuno wanted to return home as soon as possible. He also intended to put this opportunity to use on Marie's behalf. On arriving in Tokyo, he immediately contacted Asao, to discuss the film he'd been thinking about ever since he realized that Marie was seriously ill. Asao suggested that I be included in the project, so after reuniting his father with relatives in Tokushima and reserving a room for him at a hotel there, Matsuno came back to Tokyo alone.

I was meeting him for the first time, and it had been five years since I'd seen Asao. The occasion, which gave Matsuno a chance to officially inform me that Marie was beyond any hope of recovery and, on that basis, to talk about his plans for the movie, revealed a rather different person from the man Miyo, and Marie's letters, had led me to expect.

In Asao I sensed a new maturity that had come with experience, working on a succession of jobs in a position of responsibility. He was no longer the quiet, amiable youth with the smooth face of a boy in his late teens, trailing after Marie, willing to do anything for her. Certain distinctive traits in his personality had begun to emerge.

Sergio Matsuno must have been at least sixty, but was still a powerful-looking man, every inch of him baked in the Mexican sun. He had a round, fleshy face with large features and a sweeping expanse of forehead; even his pores were large, seeming like tiny wells in his ruddy skin. Most of the people I'd known during my stay in Mexico City had been intellectuals who spent their days shut up in their studies, their pallor adding to the melancholy impression they gave. Matsuno, committed to his own kind of religious activity, was undoubtedly an intellectual too, but he was also someone who got his hands dirty as he worked alongside the other people on the farm.

"If the cancer spread from a tumor in Marie's breast, as you say, then why wasn't everything possible done for her while there was still time?" my wife asked. "She'd been worried herself, and once she'd got settled, she could easily have flown to California, or even come back here for a mammogram and the necessary treatment...."

"That isn't a complicated test; they can do it in Mexico City or

Guadalajara. Indeed, the hospital where Marie is now comes up to international standards." Matsuno's rather formal way of speaking sounded a little strange to our ears. "Marie not only worked on the farm herself but saw to any health problems the other women had. Unfortunately, she didn't seem to care about her own health."

Asao had apparently already asked the same question—most likely in an accusing tone—and heard all the details from Matsuno. Knowing what he did now, he had stopped feeling bitter, consigning his initial resentment, along with any hope of early detection and treatment of Marie's cancer, to the irretrievable past. You could see that in the way he kept his eyes fixed on the floor, his head bowed in stony affirmation. I was hoping my wife would stop her accusations and retreat to the kitchen, but Matsuno clung to every word, apparently grateful for the chance to tell us how Marie had dealt with the illness.

"Looking back on it now, I feel Marie may have known she had breast cancer for years, and actually coaxed it along, encouraged it to spread. If she'd had a lover, he would have noticed the abnormality in her breast, but she lived like a nun on our farm. Even when the disease had progressed to the point where lumps had formed in various parts of her body, it seems she told no one else about it.

"And then it was too late to do anything. After she entered the hospital, she made it perfectly clear that she didn't want to be operated on, and to this day, she hasn't been. The hospital staff were angry at first, so I even went so far as to lie for her, saying that she had religious grounds for doing this, to help back her up....

"Some of the people on the farm are hoping for a miracle; they think that if her body is left untouched by the surgeon's knife, the cancer that's spread through it will suddenly disappear.

The fact is, she does have a strong life force, and at least from the outside, even in the past two or three years, she looked perfectly healthy...."

"Marie once said she'd like to go to 'the other side' before she got too old," my wife said, "while she still had her figure, without a scar or blemish. While she could still wear the same size of dress. 'In case there is another side,' she said, 'I don't want to disappoint the people who'll be waiting for me'.... She was laughing, as usual, when she said it, so I thought it was just a joke at the time.... But when she said 'people,' I'm sure she was thinking of her children...." Her voice caught in her throat, and when she stood up to leave I saw Asao, who had been keeping his distance until then, grow rigid about the neck and shoulders as he tried to control the storm of emotions inside him, waiting for it to pass.

"Marie has got very thin, but since she refuses to be operated on, of course her body is still perfect," Matsuno murmured as if to himself, then raised his heavy eyelids and looked straight at me.

I wanted to change the drift of the conversation.

"But rejecting surgery wasn't what you'd call a reasonable, well thought out decision, was it?"

"Reasonable or unreasonable ... we've done everything possible to see that her wishes are respected, in the way she's chosen," he replied, opening wide those bloodshot eyes, too big for a man his age, to stare at me again.

Asao agreed. "I doubt she'd have been able to have things her way in a Japanese hospital.... I think we should give Mr. Matsuno credit for putting up a good fight. We ought to follow his example, and handle things in a way she'd approve of. That's what the two of us have been talking about."

With steady confidence, he then told us what needed to be done from now on. As I've mentioned before, the Asao I'd known until then was a good-natured boy, always ready to respond to

Marie's impulsive (though not quite erratic) requests, taking responsibility for what he was doing, yet enjoying himself as well. But, seeing him from this new angle, it was clear that either on his Korean father's side or perhaps his mother's, there were some highly sophisticated people in his background, and for several generations back. Something in the long, square face, well suited to his close-cropped hair, and in the firm lips and clear-cut eyes, also hinted at a cold indifference to people and things that didn't really interest him.

Asao explained the decision he'd already reached in his discussion with Matsuno. At first they'd considered bringing Marie back to Japan for treatment, but it was much too late for that. All they could do now was think about how to wind up her affairs. With her mother and children gone, she had no immediate family or close relatives. But the two summer houses, one in Izukogen and the other in Komoro, were her property. Thanks to the recent explosion in land prices, they would be worth quite a lot now. Asao had shown the letter of proxy Matsuno had brought with him from Mexico to a lawyer at the company Marie's grandfather had founded, and had learned that her estate, including her stocks, could be disposed of exactly as she wanted.

Marie herself wanted to sell everything while she was still alive and donate the money to the farm. But now that he was doing well financially, Matsuno would prefer to see it invested in the production of a film to be made by Asao's team: a visual record of Marie's life. He had sounded her out on the idea before he'd left, and she had shown some interest.

"What we're proposing, K, is that you write a novel we can base the scenario on. You know her personally, and you've got a handicapped child, just as she did, so we think you're the best person for the job. When she sent you all those long letters, don't you think she had an idea you might be writing about her someday?"

178

"But aside from Marie's own feelings, I wonder, Mr. Matsuno, why you want to make her life into a film...." I was beginning to seriously consider cooperating.

"The people working on my farm, Indians and mestizos, and the Japanese from the colony in Mexico City, too, all have their faith as a common bond, but for the past five years they've also had Marie as a living symbol of it. Her presence united them for the first time, so they now all work together, sharing the hardships. But after Marie dies, where will they turn for moral support? And so I thought, if only we had a film about her to show at Sunday morning prayer sessions....

"That was how I first got the idea. But what we create out of practical necessity I expect to grow into something of far greater significance.... You know, the people on my farm now believe in Marie as a saint. If we can first show how utterly devoted she's been these past five years, which is why she came to be regarded that way ..."

"We're going to Mexico with our cameras," Asao said. "If we make the rounds of everyone on the farm, from the old people down to the children, first Indians and mestizos, then Japanese, we should pick up some amazing eyewitness accounts. We want to use our microphones and cameras to collect stories about her as a saint, like the ones in the medieval Legend of the Holy Grail. Seems funny to be calling her a saint, though...."

"But that's how everyone on the farm thinks of her. There are many women in Cacoyagua who have been called saints, it's that sort of place.... I can imagine how she'd react, though, if someone called her 'Saint Marie' to her face; she'd laugh in that way she has—like a bright, sunny day....

"You know, when she first accepted my proposal to come and work with us, under my direction so to speak, it was as a person destined to become a saint. I admit it myself: I asked her to act that way, but everything she did was perfectly natural.... It all started at the commune in California, where I heard what had happened to her children. I asked her to play the part of someone who was enduring the pain of a terrible loss, and had come all the way to Mexico to devote her life to god. I then told the people on the farm how she had lost her children. A disaster there's no way of making up for, but a story that's very real to us in Mexico, even among people with very little education.

"The young girls on our farm—it's hard to tell if they're ever serious or not, they all seem to have sex on the brain—yet even they were moved. They come from deep in the mountains, where you can get stung by a scorpion if you're not careful, and go to the missionaries to learn to read and write. After a civilized life in the dormitory at school, they don't fit in back home any more, so down they go to Mexico City. And they soon find that all they can do there is go to work as maids or prostitutes.... The priest brings them to us, hoping we'll make respectable women of them....

"As even these girls well know, Marie is a suffering mother who came to the Mexican countryside to find some spiritual comfort in self-sacrifice; she has made everyone believe in that role. And nothing could have been more natural for her. For it's all true—the experience is hers, and even the reason for coming to Mexico to work on the farm, as well. All she had to do was live her own life, and mingle with the people around her, just as she is. After a while I myself couldn't understand why I went to all that trouble, begging her to come....

"But then when I first met her in California, and later again in Mexico City, her cheerfulness was so natural. No trace of despair over the trouble she was having at the time, nor even over her children's deaths."

I reminded myself that in Mexico City, while he was talking her into coming to the farm, they had argued about religion—I knew that from Marie's letter—and that Matsuno had long been involved in church activities. But here he seemed to have stopped trying to interpret her life in terms of religion, presenting himself as just a simple, honest farmer, stunned with grief.

I turned next to Asao, and asked him for his thoughts about Marie.

"I was barely twenty then … and I'd never known a woman like her, so well educated and yet so cheerful and easygoing, never letting little things bother her. As you know, the three of us were always together, and she was an older woman, and beautiful, too. Not that the relationship was explicitly sexual, but, looking back on it now, when we were with her there was a sexy feeling in the air. It felt good just being able to do things for her. And all the time we were having fun together, she was educating us.

"We even stuck our noses into that sexual fix she got herself into, and did what we could to get her out of it. There aren't many guys in their early twenties who get a chance to do something like that for an older, intellectual woman…. We were so young then, we never imagined she could have this dark, murky side to her when it came to sex…. She was embarrassed about it, but found it pretty funny, too, and all the time that guy with the tape was really throwing her for a loop. And there we were on the sidelines, trying to be helpful. Of course it was you, K, who actually worked out what was going on….

"What happened next wasn't just a bit of high-risk hanky-panky, but her children's deaths…. After that, we were utterly helpless. It was as though we were the ones who'd taken the blow. We couldn't find anything to say to comfort her, just stood by watching from a distance. Planning to jump in and help if she even hinted she needed us, and we did help her a little, I guess….

"It changed her. Afterward we could always see the pain, pressing down on her like a great weight. I often thought it must be a tremendous job for her just to stay alive. I felt a new respect for her, different from before; and every time I saw her it seemed *she* was encouraging *me*. I found myself thinking that someday we'd have to do something big enough to measure up to what she was going through....

"That's been on our minds for the last five years, ever since she went away. We've been waiting, thinking if we just sat tight and kept improving, one day she'd send for us, but this time to work with her on a real, adult job, not like the stuff we used to do for her.

"... I never dreamed Marie'd be suffering from terminal cancer. Or that we'd be filming a record of her life, with the help of some Mexicans who see her as a saint. But now that I've actually seen the plan, I feel that what we've been doing over the years to prepare ourselves has been right.... Marie always gave the impression of being swept along by some power outside herself, when basically she was the axis things revolved around. I think that's true this time, too; that she's the one who created this opportunity for us, to do our first real work...."

Around that time, Asao's team had been shooting special programs for television. They were now working on a series for a well-known producer (even I had heard of him) who specialized in serious documentaries, and who made a point of hiring people from outside the studio to improve the quality of episodes filmed on location abroad. But Asao was ready to cancel the contract and leave for Mexico immediately with his two friends.

"A famous producer like that won't let you off so easily right in the middle of a project, will he?" I asked; to which Asao responded with a sneer that told me at once how freelancers regard producers employed by TV stations. He and his friends must have been about thirty by then, but they were all still unmarried, free to go where they liked.

With the talk about work settled for the time being, we started drinking, and for the first time in quite a while I had some beer. Matsuno, who didn't take long to get drunk, changed from the simple, hardworking, practical man he'd seemed in front of my wife, and began at last to resemble the person I had encountered in Marie's letters. He told us of the vision he had—one I've already mentioned: of taking this film we were about to make with Marie as the protagonist and showing it on an outdoor screen in villages around the Mexican countryside; adding that he'd like the title to be "The Last Woman in the World," apparently determined to persuade Asao and me to go along with this idea. Asao, too, as he downed drink after drink at a surprising rate, started saying things with a rather different slant from what he'd outlined for us not long before. And when she brought us something to eat, my wife also joined in again, as a listener; it was Matsuno and Asao who did most of the talking. Some of the things I remember them saying during our long drinking session, particularly those that seemed to reveal their inner selves, are worth recording.

Sergio Matsuno:

"I was brought up in the Christian faith, which my grandfather passed down to us, and I still believe in it. That's one reason why I started my farming project. But of course as a religious activist, I am only an amateur; I've had no training for the priesthood. My sister, though, became a nun, joining the local branch of St. Francis Xavier's order, which is well known here in Japan.

"We have a chapel on the farm, where the priest gives us instruction and we all pray together. And yet Marie seemed reluctant to join in, even in these simple services. When my sister paid occasional visits to the farm, it used to annoy her. Marie almost never came to the chapel, and even when she did, she would often just sit there and watch the other women pray. But everyone loved and respected her a lot more than they ever did my sister; they even came to regard her as a saint. There was a certain aura about her that seemed to say, 'I may not share your beliefs, but I'm not one to look down on those who pray.' And underneath this was a woman who had suffered a terrible tragedy.

"In the beginning I asked her to let the people around her know, through her presence, that she had no intention of hiding her grief, but was working among us to ease it; and yet I never asked her to believe as we do. I had no right to. But over time, in her own way, which she perhaps learned at the Center she once belonged to, Marie's own form of prayer got deeper. This, too, everyone seemed to sense. When she was alone, I believe she was praying all the time.

"Marie has cancer, and is dying, as the saint of Cacoyagua Farm.... Knowing this was like being hit over the head, and it forced me to think again about belief.... Her sons died a hideous death. Thoughts of it haunted her, and there was no escape—for her, this was reality. To forget the pain and sadness, she worked hard, not for herself but for other people. There was no lie in this, either, but when I asked her to come to the farm, I suggested she tell herself she was playing a part. And then—turning what began as an act into the real thing, played out on the stage of life and death, with no way out—the cancer appeared....

"Before we were aware of it, Marie had accepted it, and was prepared to die, all the while continuing to devote herself to the young women on the farm. From her hospital bed, she still thinks of them. Those who go to visit her come back encouraged themselves. Everyone is saying she's a saint. Rumors about her have spread, and now women from other villages want to go to see her too, so many that the hospital has had to limit her visitors.

"... Near death herself, Marie still worries about the poor women on the farm. She has left everything she owns to us, as the whole village knows, though we don't intend to use it for ourselves. All the preparations—for dying a saint's death—have been made. And I like to think it's god who made them. What Marie herself would say about that, though, I don't know ... for even now I sometimes can't tell what she really feels.

"… I have always believed in god, ever since I was a child, and I've spent my life trying to lead what you might call a religious movement, in my own way. But never before have I felt so clearly, 'Ah! This is the power of god at work.' Ever since I was introduced to Marie in California, I've acted as though I were the one with experience in matters of belief, and if someone were to accuse me of using her for my movement in Cacoyagua, I would have to admit they were right. But I like to think that god revealed himself to her, not me. If I tried to tell that to Marie herself, though, she would probably ask how a fatal illness like cancer can be divine providence, and say that it didn't make sense, that none of this was 'intelligible.' That's just the way she is.…"

Asao:
"After Musan and Michio died, I think Marie taught us more than she ever had before, by confronting her loss the way she did. Japan was all peace and prosperity when we were growing up, and we knew we could get by without putting ourselves out too much, but then we couldn't see much meaning in life, either. We knew we weren't cut out to be respectable cogs in the corporate wheel that keeps society going. Didn't want to be, either.

"So since we'd pretty much given up on the future anyway, we made up our minds not to do any kind of work we didn't want to. We'd settled into a conservative-pessimist frame of mind, and didn't seem likely to go beyond it. She cheerfully put up with us, not that we forced ourselves on her. She was easygoing, always ready for a good time.

"But then when her children killed themselves we saw Marie, who'd never seemed to have a care in the world, somehow managing to survive under that crushing burden, and that's when we started to think maybe we should take our own lives a bit more seriously. Remember the time when she was so depressed after the play that Filipino group put on? Well, I wanted to give her at least some of the encouragement she'd given us, so I told her what she'd meant to us since the Izu thing. She said, 'The worst thing imaginable has happened to me, and I'm still alive—it's enough to make you think there's no meaning in life after all, isn't it?' and then laughed, for the first time in I don't know how long....

"Anyway, we want to go to Mexico and see her while she can still talk. We could've gone before—all we had to do was catch a plane for Mexico City—but we were afraid Marie'd disapprove. I could just hear her saying, 'I've finally found a new life—why do you have to come chasing after me?' We were barely twenty when we met her, so I guess we've always been a bit overawed by her.

"... But now everything's set, and we're finally leaving for Mexico with our cameras and microphones. That doesn't mean we think there was some superhuman power getting things ready for us behind the scenes, though...."

Ten days before Sergio Matsuno, who had to wait for his father, Asao and his group left for Mexico City. Matsuno had called the farm in Cacoyagua and arranged for them to be met at the airport, then taken to the hospital in Guadalajara. The first letter from the film crew arrived the day Matsuno left Japan with his father.

Considering how unforthcoming he'd once been, Asao's description of the situation there was surprisingly long and detailed. But what startled me when I opened the flimsy airmail envelope were the two polaroid color pictures he'd enclosed. They were obviously the work of a professional, and looked as if they might be stills for the film.

The first was of Marie lying propped up in a hospital bed. Her face was much darker now, and her hair, grown so thin it was frizzy, was drawn tightly back, revealing the fine shape of her skull. But the red lips, the winning smile, and the eyes—even bigger than before, the shadows darker—were just as I remembered them. Wearing a negligee, she held her right hand in front of her now perfectly flat chest, the fingers—whatever this gesture may have meant—open in a V sign, as one often sees children doing....

The other had been taken in a dark corridor, which accounted for its slightly murky quality, despite the use of professional lighting. A crowd of Indian women were huddled in a corner, squatting on the stone floor. With eyes that shone blue in the light but must have been brown or black, they stared up anxiously at the camera, holding bouquets of gladioli, carnations, and cattleyas across their bent knees. Herded into a basement hallway, worry and fatigue showing plainly in their faces, they were apparently determined to wait.

Asao wrote:

> *Marie seemed in better shape than we'd imagined from what Sergio told us. All three of us got to talk to her. Only for a little while, though.... She has good days and bad days, and at the hospital they said they'd have to see what effect our visit had on her, so we couldn't make a definite appointment for the next time.*
>
> *The first thing she said when she saw us was, "What're you guys doing here?!" Sergio may have told her it was you he'd be bringing back. But then again, maybe that was just a typical Marie-style greeting. Anyway, when we told her we were still together, working as a film crew now, she seemed pleased. She already knew you were going to write something for the movie, and said, "Even if it's about me, what K writes will be his own story, one acceptable to him—it's only natural, isn't it?" She also seemed concerned about the title, and warned us not to go along with any fancy idea that might pop into Sergio's head. She herself prefers "Parientes de la Vida," an expression she's heard the local women use in times of trouble.*
>
> *She doesn't look all that bad, but her voice is terribly weak,*

barely audible. It must have been a tremendous effort for her to talk that much. We thought filming would be too hard on her, so we just took one snapshot before we left. Then our guide told us there was a group of women from the farm in Cacoyagua in the underground passageway between the hospital buildings, and took us to see them. We took a picture there, too, but we were told they wouldn't be allowed in to see Marie, and it's against hospital rules for her to accept any bouquets. Actually, Marie's room was so bare it was like a laboratory, or a storeroom.

The people from the farm had booked us into a hotel near the museum in Guadalajara, so we'll be starting work soon, using the hotel as a base. I'll keep you posted. We were talking among ourselves about how dark Marie's got—just like a Mexican peasant—when our Japanese-Mexican guide told us she was much darker before, and that in the three months she's been in the hospital she's actually gone back to looking Japanese. I'm enclosing the snapshot we took, so you can see what you think. She's a little paler than she looks in the picture, though....

Marie was right: I *have* turned her life into "my own story, one acceptable to me." And there's a gap of five years I know nothing about. Did she finally come to see the world as 'intelligible' during those years or not—who knows? Even if I went all the way to the hospital in Guadalajara, I don't believe she'd tell me, assuming I managed to ask. A smile might appear on her Betty Boop face, now much darker than before, but I expect she would remain silent, the shadows around her eyes only deeper still. I doubt she'd even give me the V sign I saw in the polaroid photo. So, with this picture and its enigmatic gesture as a clue, I can only offer my portrait of Marie facing death alone in Mexico as a conclusion to "my own story." I know from experience that people who write about human life as "their own story" seldom see it as 'intelligible' themselves. But for me everything in this story has

188

led toward that scene: of Marie on her deathbed, giving that mysterious V sign with one thin, dark hand, and with a certain radiance in her smile....

For the final shot in the film I'm helping Asao and his friends to make, I want them to use this photograph of Marie in her hospital room. I believe Asao took it with that in mind. I think of the Indians and mestizos Sergio Matsuno told us about when he was drunk, waiting for the end of the world, staring up at this picture on an outdoor screen.

The phrase Marie suggested using as a title, "Parientes de la Vida"—assuming that Asao got the Spanish right and wrote it down correctly—can be translated as "relatives in life." As I interpreted it, it meant that she was proud in a modest sort of way to have been accepted by the local women as one of them, a true friend who had shared in their suffering and, though not a blood relation, had become part of the family. And, bearing this in mind, I tried to see a link between this feeling and the V sign in the photograph, her weak but unmistakable gesture....

But then recently, one night when I couldn't sleep, I came across a passage in a paperback edition of Plutarch where he refers to sadness as an unwelcome "relative in life" that nobody ever gets rid of, no matter what situation they're in. I'm now leaning toward this view of it. Either way, as they watch the film of Marie's life, the Mexican countrywomen should be able to take in the meaning of "Parientes de la Vida" just as it is.

In lieu of an epilogue

A young woman who works for a publishing company was supposed to bring me two videotapes back from Mexico, where she'd spent her New Year's holiday. But one of them was confiscated at customs, or perhaps just held for a time, so I don't have it yet. Will it be lost forever, before I have a chance to see how the plot develops after the tape I do have ends? This worries me a lot, but the girl's explanation wasn't clear. In fact, being very serious and only around twenty or so, she was terribly upset with me for the unexpected trouble she'd run into at the airport, and stood in the doorway spluttering, "I was almost arrested for smuggling pornography!" refusing even to come inside.

Left holding a paper bag, which seemed somehow off-balance with only one cassette inside, I thought: "What the hell?!" and then again: "What's the use?!" I already have some idea of what's on the film I can't actually see, and I'm sure it's not pornographic. But even if I'd been there, standing beside the customs officer as he peered at the TV screen, spot-checking it (or whatever they do —perhaps even watching it all, from beginning to end), I doubt I would have been able to defend it convincingly.

The screen would have shown a hospital room, bare as a factory research lab. A Japanese woman in her mid-forties, lying on the bed. After a while, darkness. No one is allowed to tamper with the wiring, so they haven't used any lighting equipment, and when an afternoon shower breaks, the interior, even the sky behind the cameraman's back, turns black as night. The camera keeps running, though, for their time is limited, and they want to record the pounding of the rain and the crack of thunder, with an occasional flash of lightning illuminating the room.

In the letter that just came, Asao says he had the camera on his shoulder, shooting into the darkness, his back drenched from the spray of raindrops coming through the window he'd opened a crack to catch the sound. As he stood there shivering, he heard a rustling from the bed, dark even to the naked eye. He stopped the camera and waited in silence for a while, but when—in one of those sudden changes so typical of early autumn weather in Mexico—daylight poured into the room again, he was back in position with the camera running. But what appeared in his lens this time, and in the eyes of the entire crew, was Marie's body, the sheet thrown off, stark naked.

She was little more than a skeleton—the only ornament in the room was a handmade tin skeleton taking a bath by her pillow—but there wasn't a mark on the dark, sleek skin. Stretched out on the bed, she was exploring the edges of her oddly luxuriant muff of pubic hair with the thumb and forefinger of her left hand. As if to unnerve these three young friends she'd known so long, she was holding her right hand in a V sign at her chest, the hint of a smile on her face. Asao kept the camera focused on the naked body of this woman dying of cancer until the film ran out....

The second video was in color, just as the first would have been, but that was hard to tell from the bleak, monochrome scene that appeared on the screen when I played it back. It was dark and out of focus, and made me wonder if this was the best Asao and his friends could do, for although I had known them for ten years now, I had never actually seen their work, aside from a few snapshots.

Even so, as my eyes searched the screen, from out of the silence I could hear even, regular strokes, digging—or, rather, gouging out—a hole in the stony earth. At the same time, I caught sight of a figure, the movements of a human torso, far off in the distance on the dimly lit screen. Beneath a cloudy evening sky, in the midst of a wasteland, a man is standing on a slope, digging. The camera is below him, and focused solely on the up-and-down motion of the hoe swung by this man with legs so unnaturally stiff they seem unrelated to the supple strength of his upper body. But with the camera trained on the swinging hoe, it's possible to see the entire scene—monotonous and blurry as it is—in detail, as though you were looking at a still photograph.

In the top left-hand corner is the wall of a church (the upper part, the roof and bell tower, is out of the picture), made of stone or brick, covered with stucco. Scattered over the gentle slope on this side of it, in darkness where the shadow cuts across, are what at first appear to be the remains of some ruined shacks. But then, realizing that these are gravestones, I quickly grasp the situation.

The cemetery covers the entire hillside, from the top, where the church is, down to the lower right-hand corner of the screen. It is barren land, devoid of any plant life except for an occasional willow, black and withered. Some distance away from where most of the tombstones are grouped, and yet as though this place, a level spot halfway down the slope, had been specially set aside for him, the man is digging a grave, alone.

Further down the hill, below the man swinging his hoe—I repeat myself, but he's the only living thing in the vast area shown on the screen—a stone wall about the height of a person's thigh cuts across the rocky wasteland. On this side of it is a muddy path, trodden into a deep, pitch-black furrow in the earth, with the video camera apparently positioned on another stone wall in front of it.

The man still swings his hoe. As the hole gets deeper, every movement makes his lower limbs appear more awkward, as though the bones were broken and had healed badly: legs so rigid the knees might have been encased in steel plates, but incredibly massive and powerful. The torso is equally solid, but moves with a supple force. He stands facing the church, showing the camera his broad, muscular back, thick neck, and huge head, bowed as he works. I thought at first he might be a Mexican wrestler—the kinky, tousled hair, clinging to the skull, adds to that impression—but when he rests his hoe on the ground and twists around, straining to hear some distant sound, the profile shown in the white light slipping through the evening clouds is so clearly Japanese, even from a distance, that I catch my breath and look again....

By the time the microphone picks up the rumbling in the earth—countless hooves hammering on dirt and gravel—the man has resumed his solitary digging. The camera is still trained on him when a mass of dark, blurred shapes passes in front of it, a herd of cows, pushing and jostling their way down the black, muddy path. The image on the screen wobbles violently here, as the startled cameraman moves backward on the wall. This is where the first scene ends.

In the scene that immediately follows it, it is still evening, in a corner of the same barren stretch of land, but the camera is now pointed down, focused on what look like two brightly colored eyes, one red and the other green, peering out from beneath a thin layer of earth on top of the gravel. (Here I realized for the first time that the film was in color.) A square of bright metal touches the eyes, then disappears beneath them, and the red and green balls come popping out, covered with dirt. The hoe has unearthed the fruit (or perhaps the buds) of a certain kind of cactus. Then laughter—two or three people obviously from Tokyo—joined one beat later by laughter of a different kind, oddly nervous, inconsistent with the booming, throaty voice. Still laughing, the voice (I remember hearing Mexicans of Japanese descent talk this way—simple and honest on the surface, but with a mocking undertone) goads these city boys on: "EAT IT! IT'S SWEET, SO EAT IT! MAYBE YOU GET THE TROTS, BUT NOT SO BAD. OR SPOTS ON YOUR FACE, BUT JUST A FEW. IT'S REALLY GOOD, SO GO ON, TRY IT!"

It is darker in the next scene, which takes place on that same level patch halfway up the slope, but the images, filmed at close range, are sharp and clear. The figure with the hoe—a giant of a man, aged thirty-five or -six, dwarfing everyone around him—is hard at work again, surrounded now by Japanese-Mexicans, mestizos, and Indians, children among them, all eagerly pitching in. The grave is now a sharply outlined rectangle, deep enough for the bottom of it to be pitch dark....

In the letter from Mexico, the only explanation concerning the contents of this second video was that the filming of preparations for Marie's funeral had gone badly at first, but picked up later on. This was typical of Asao and his crew, for both in speaking and writing they generally used as few words as possible, perhaps because they could only think of self-expression in terms of videos and movies. Yet ever since I first got to know them, this reluctance to fall back on language has made me trust them all the more. Giving the film they bring back with them words, in fact—helping with the editing, shaping it—will be my job (though there's still customs to worry about, of course).

So what I'm adding here is only a rough sketch of that part of the story which began to take shape as I watched the video. Underlying it is certain information the film crew don't yet have. This is what I'll base my sketch on, but it was watching those scenes, over and over again, that actually pulled the story together in my mind....

Let me start, though, by reviewing the setting. Behind where the video camera was, the slope continues down to a ravine where a river flows during the rainy season, with another hill rising on the other side. In reverse, this gentle slope grows into a steep mountain with an Aztec pyramid near the top, but part of the way up, nestled in the hillside, is an old village. The graveyard and adjoining church that appeared on the video are on its outskirts, set apart from the village, which is centered around another church, one the people living there built themselves with stones they hauled down from the pyramid. On the tract of land between the two churches (the whole area, including the ravine, was a ranch before the war) lies the cooperative farm. This has a chapel of its own, but comes under the direct supervision of the local parish, to which it has donated a fixed percentage of its income from the flowers and vegetables sold in Mexico City since becoming financially viable.

In the notes they drew up after arriving in Mexico, the film crew included a report on the present circumstances of the farm. This mentioned that, although it would be possible to get by without knowing any Spanish—the manager, Sergio Matsuno, was a second-generation Mexican of Japanese descent, but fluent in Japanese, and about a third of the workers were also the children or grandchildren of immigrants from the Japanese colony in Mexico City—the lifestyle was purely Mexican, and with the villagers to deal with every day as well, it seemed incredible that a woman from Japan had actually lived there for five years.

Marie's various activities were described in an article in the newspaper printed in Guadalajara, the nearest city; I have a copy of the clipping with me. According to this, besides working on the farm, she had volunteered as a social worker, dealing mainly with health care for women, both on the farm and in the community at large. The article was a long piece, and with my level of Spanish I could only skim through it; yet even taking the florid prose so typical of local Mexican papers into account, it's clear that Marie had actually saved the people there from what might have been a major disaster.

She had discovered that a considerable number of the women working on the farm showed symptoms of tuberculosis. After they'd been sent to the hospital in Guadalajara for treatment, she took quick and decisive action. First, she found out that all these women lived in the village, not the farm, and all were mothers with children ranging from babies to ones of school age. A portable X-ray machine was brought in a truck from Guadalajara, and tests revealed that many of the village children, in addition to those whose mothers were infected, were suffering from TB. People jumped to conclusions—it was the hard labor that gave these women the disease, which they then spread to their children—and were quick to accuse the outsider, the manager of the farm.

But through her own investigation, Marie proved this hasty judgment to be untrue. An elderly American woman writer had bought a sprawling house in the old section near the church, which she'd had remodeled inside, leaving the adobe exterior and surrounding wall untouched. She had a spacious living room, which she'd offered to the farm workers as a private day care center, and other children gathered there to play as well. Every child in the village had been in and out of her house at one time or another. The woman disapproved of the way the village church ran its Sunday school, and was vehemently opposed to the "Japanese-style management" of the farm.

Naturally it was she who led the attack on the farm when the TB epidemic came to light. Marie took sole responsibility for these accusations, and after paying repeated visits to her large house in the center of town, finally uncovered the fact that the old lady herself had contracted tuberculosis half a century before, and was now suffering from a recurrence of it. Her infection measured 8 on the Gaffky scale, which was very serious. When she realized that she'd been the unwitting source of the children's illness, the woman used her own money to save as many of them as possible. Marie did everything she could to help, and in a short time they stopped the disease from spreading any further, though three babies died.

For Marie, this incident must have been particularly painful. The long journey to reconstruct her inner life that ended in this village in Mexico had started with the deaths of her own children. And yet through the process of saving these other children's lives, she came to be regarded as a saint, not only by the women on the farm and in the village, but throughout the area.

A living saint. Examples showing how this reputation grew can be found not only in the newspaper article but in the diary Sergio Matsuno let me see. But when I tried to give a clear account of it myself in the first draft of this book, I ended up deleting it all at a later stage. How *is* a modern saint created? It seemed the harder I worked at describing this process—the more concrete details I added—the more "?'s" appeared beside the lines I was writing.

I once read the English translation of Vargas Llosa's *The War of the End of the World*, which came out before I started writing this; the Brazilian writer Nelrida Piñon recommended it to me when we were both working in the same program at an American university—the author's dedication to her appears on the title page. I found Llosa's description of a struggle waged by a religious community against the military authorities believable, down to the last detail. Disappointing, however, was the portrait of the Counsellor who leads the fight against "the Anti-Christ"; his character never seemed to develop beyond the brief sketch at the beginning of the novel. So although I was moved when I finished reading it, at a more basic level I felt I'd been cheated, which made me realize how badly I'd wanted some evidence of the Counsellor's "mystery." I wrote about this in a letter to Nelrida, who had since become a friend, and received a postcard in reply from São Paolo: "You're a year older than I am, aren't you, K? Honestly, it brings tears to my eyes to think you're still going through life like a little lost lamb!"—this, intended to be sympathetic, I suppose, but delivered with the caustic humor typical of South American women.

The fact is, though, that because I have no real belief, in any sense of the word, I find it impossible to approach the concept of a saint in my own writing, just as I found it impossible to accept the Counsellor in someone else's work. And, despite my age, I'm afraid I *am* like a "lost lamb" wandering in a daze, unable to lift my feelings above this emptiness deep inside me....

Marie, having known this side of me for years, sent me the sign of a saint in her easy, casual way—making a V sign as children often do, with her thin right hand held at her flat chest— before dying in that hospital in Guadalajara and being buried in the graveyard next to the church in her Mexican village. A giant of a man with stiff, awkward legs but enormous power in his upper body had dug her grave alone, until he was joined by a crowd of Japanese-Mexicans, mestizos, and Indians, who, though they had banned him from the place until then, were now reconciled with him and, to show it, helped finish digging the grave. This was the series of events recorded on the video.

I came across the following passage when I was leafing through Sergio Matsuno's diary. The content in itself was shocking, but the fact that he hadn't even hinted at it when he was telling us about Marie's cancer made it doubly so.

> *Seems Macho Mitsuo raped Marie. For three months now, Mitsuo and his gang have been raising hell. Now it's clear that when they came tearing in on their motorbikes they'd had their sights on Marie. / Mitsuo raped Marie again. It happened while we were in the chapel. Young Jorge was standing guard outside Marie's room. Mitsuo threw him out into the courtyard, flat on his back. He got up again right away and came to the chapel to tell us, so we ran to help. By the time we got there, no sign of either Mitsuo or his bike. Aguiella, who was giving the greenhouse an airing at the time, says that Mitsuo was in Marie's room for about three minutes. / Apparently Mitsuo was boasting to his gang at the cantina that it only took Marie three minutes to come. Anyway, their stories match. Must be careful to keep the rumor from spreading. Mitsuo is at his mother's place in the village. There's no guarantee he won't try it again.*

The entries recording the two rapes appear within three days of each other. For a while there's no mention of either Marie or Mitsuo, and then, four weeks later, two more entries related to the incident follow, dated a day apart.

> *Saw Marie sitting on a bench in the chapel this morning, and it isn't even Sunday. She looked pale but rested. Greeted me in English: "Rejoice!" But said she was going to take the afternoon off. / Eight men from the farm summoned Macho Mitsuo and beat him up, crushing both his kneecaps. Destroyed his bike, too. Forced his gang to swear they'd never show their faces around the farm again, and let them go. But when he's recovered, who's to say he won't be back to get revenge? For sheer brute strength, there's nobody to match him—even two, or three, to one. But the priest has said he'll never allow the men on the farm to arm themselves. / Have forbidden Marie to talk to the authorities*

about anything concerning Mitsuo. If the police are called in she'll have to tell them she was raped, and once that happens there'll be no stopping the rumors. It would be front-page news, even in Mexico City. And that would make not only the farm but the whole country a difficult place for Marie to be. / Marie said if Mitsuo was beaten that badly, he'll never be back, even when his wounds heal. The reason—that he's a real macho. But won't his being so macho make him all the more reluctant to lie low, like a whipped dog, all the more determined to get revenge? Marie said: "The men were so scared he'd try to get even, they beat him till he was more dead than alive. No macho, precisely because he's a macho, can take that much violence for so long without his power to fight back being cut off at the source. I don't think he'll come back. And if he does, the gang that's been tagging along behind him won't be enough, he'll have to raise a private army. If he went that far, our men would all have to run for it, to Mexico City. But that won't happen."

I remember what Matsuno said when I met him in Tokyo: "The way Marie lived while she was in Mexico reminded me of a nun, an old-style one, dressed in a rough habit. Once we started our work on the farm, there were a lot of young guys around, and considering how aggressive Mexican men in their prime can be, not to mention hot-blooded kids, if Marie had been the slightest bit loose, things would have got completely out of hand. It was because Marie had cut off all wordly desire, just like a nun, that our project succeeded."

I also remember the following passage from the letter Marie sent me when she'd made up her mind to join the farm:

... I've decided to go on from here to Sergio Matsuno's farm, but, thinking about it, I realize that I've actually just let things happen as usual. Matsuno was so persistent, and I didn't have any plans for the time being, so I let him talk me into it. This is the

way I've always done things, but still, I also wanted proof that there's at least one thing I've decided by my own will. So, after giving it a lot of thought, I've vowed never to have sex again, as long as I live. I don't know whom I'm making this vow to except myself, since I don't have a god to believe in.... Smoking and drinking don't have any attraction for me, and I couldn't think of anything else it would be painful to give up, so I've decided to swear off sex....

Marie lost two handicapped children at once, and in a brutal way, before leaving Japan and finally joining the cooperative farm in her search for a way to recover from that loss. So when I read about the rapes in Matsuno's diary, my first, horrifying thought was, what if it had made her pregnant? I wondered if pregnancy might have been behind that "Rejoice!"—her greeting to Matsuno in the chapel four weeks after the event—particularly as Marie almost never went to mass with the others on the farm. Every time I thought of that blank four-week period, the sense of dread returned. And though I can't explain how exactly, the fact that the men from the farm waited a month before punishing the perpetrator also seemed connected to the possibility of pregnancy.

Macho: someone who flaunts his excessive masculinity; characterized by "aggressiveness, insensitivity, invulnerability".... When I was in Mexico, partly because I worked at the Colegio, the Mexicans I came to know weren't in any way like those one finds in Hollywood movies—cheerful, fiesta-loving, sly rascals who turn out to be good-hearted in the end. As I've already said, they were for the most part gloomy intellectuals. I had to turn to a book by Octavio Paz, which I used as a sort of primer on Mexican life, to learn about the macho type. And yet if I superimpose the character Matsuno refers to as Macho Mitsuo on the image I saw in the video, of that gargantuan Japanese-Mexican with crippled legs, I feel—again for no definite reason, but I'm sure I'm right— that this is the very type of macho who at bullfights in the arena at the north end of the Avenida de los Insurgentes, or at international soccer matches shown live on television, could always be seen whipping the fans into a frenzy.

Paz writes that the macho's childish innocence and stupid, even absurd jokes usually end in sinister laughter. Wasn't that episode with the cactus fruit (or buds) typical of that sort of thing, where something known to cause mild diarrhea was forced on an unsuspecting film crew from Japan?

Macho Mitsuo not only raped Marie but demonstrated his male prowess by making her come in just three minutes the second time, and with no man strong enough to stand up to him alone, he terrorized the farm. He must also have known that, given Marie's image and the effect it had on the other farm laborers, they were unlikely to let the police—and thus the local press—know what happened. This was a country where if a child were sexually assaulted and murdered by a psychopath, a picture of the blood-smeared, half-naked corpse taken at the scene would probably cover the front page of the evening edition. But equally, when the men at the farm joined forces against him and broke his knees, Mitsuo—just as Marie predicted—never considered going to the police, let alone appearing at the farm again, even when he was well enough to walk. And so time passed. . . .

On hearing of Marie's death, however, Mitsuo returns from the slums of Mexico City to his mother's place and, though his legs are still stiff, puts all the strength in the rest of his body into digging her grave with a hoe. The farmers daren't go near him, seeing this man they punished holding a possible weapon in his hands. I could imagine them cowering behind the film crew, watching. Asao, unaware of these past events, keeps his camera on him as he hacks out a hole in the ground. Then a herd of cattle intrudes, being driven home from the meager pastureland. Macho Mitsuo comes down for a closer look when he sees how rattled the film people are. An exchange ensues in Japanese, followed by the practical joke involving cactus fruit (or buds). Cautiously, the farmers draw near, and peace is made. Immigrants, Indians, mestizos—men, women, and children—join in to dig the hole where Marie will be buried....

This is how I see part of the narrative developing, as a basis for the reels of film Asao and his friends should be bringing back with them any day now. What brings both sides together in this episode is Marie's influence over them. When, driven into a corner by a bully none of them can fight alone, the farmers unite, not to kill him but to crush his kneecaps with rocks until the memory of being himself a victim is so deeply engraved that nothing can erase it, isn't it the strength these men got from Marie that prevents them from running away, after waiting in suspense since the day they left him lying injured? And isn't it Mitsuo's inability to forget the woman he raped and brought to orgasm in a mere three minutes, during his time alone in the city without even his bike (which he wouldn't have been able to ride anyway), that makes him return to dig her grave on learning of her death? A return to the people he once fought against, and is soon reconciled with....

I had already read Sergio Matsuno's diary when I started writing about Marie's life, but I left out the part about her rape because, as I mentioned, I couldn't give it any firm reality. Yet now that I've seen the figure of that giant, wielding his hoe in a barren field under a cloudy Mexican evening sky, there's nothing holding me back from telling this story, too. And so....

But something else stops me in my tracks. For if the customs people were to return the video of Marie lying there like a Naked Maja giving the V sign, wouldn't something crucial perhaps happen to me when I saw it? If, through the preparations for her own burial, the dead Marie could act as a mediator between Mitsuo and the farm, mightn't she also intercede between me and something else, by carefully staging this final image of herself in life? I know how farfetched it may sound, but it makes my heart pound with the same dread those men must have felt after they'd summoned Mitsuo and crippled him.

"They got together to fight back against someone far stronger than themselves. Have you ever done something like that?" a gentle voice might ask. And I would be obliged to say: "I have already written a novel about Marie's life, as 'my own story, one acceptable to me'...."